AGNES' GIFT

A HEARTWARMING STORY
ABOUT THE POWER OF THE ROSARY

Kristelle Angelli

D0967454

John Paul Publishing
Tewksbury, Massachusetts

John Paul Publishing
Post Office Box 283
Tewksbury, MA 01876
www.KristelleAngelli.com

Book Layout ©2013 BookDesignTemplates.com

Ordering Information:
Quantity sales. Special discounts are available on quantity purchases.
For details, contact the author at the address above.

Agnes' Gift/Kristelle Angelli. -- 1st ed.
ISBN 978-0-9981575-0-4

*To my mother and father, and to all the strong women
in my family, especially my grandmothers.*

CHAPTER ONE

Introduction

Through the sea was your path; your way, through the mighty waters, though your footsteps were unseen (Psalm 77:20).

Warm inside her living room and safe from the bitter cold that comes with a December night in Boston, Jenna was lying under the artificial tree that had been part of Christmas in her family for as long as she could remember. She found comfort in the familiar colored lights and the various handmade and store-bought ornaments that faithfully found their way onto the tree each year. With all the changes taking place in her life, the tree's glow not only brought warmth to the room, but it also seemed to permeate her heart, bringing a sense of well-being that was a welcomed relief from the unrest that had become a familiar companion.

Every year, Jenna looked forward to unpacking those ornaments and allowing the memory each one carried to comfort her with a sense of tradition and stability. Each was like a thread that weaved together the good times of her past, bringing them into the present like a warm blanket covering and protecting her.

Jenna was halfway through her junior year in high school. This year in particular she welcomed that connection to past years, which reminded her who she was and where she had been. It brought with it the feeling that she could face the uncertain times ahead and maybe even find her way in a world that felt increasingly unpredictable and out of control.

As Jenna scanned the Christmas tree, her gaze settled on a seashell hanging in the center, a souvenir from Cape Cod where her family rented a beach house each summer. She thought back to those endless summer afternoons the year she and her older brother, Justin, had learned to windsurf. They spent more time crashing into the water than standing on the sailboard. Just below the seashell was an ornament cut out of felt that she made in first grade, hanging next to the one Justin made. Jenna's was a lopsided red bow, while Justin's was a perfectly proportioned snowman. Seeing the two side by side made it obvious that Justin was the artist in the family. On the other side of the tree was the wooden angel that her grandpa carved for her when she was little. He had glued a photo of her four-year-old face on the face of the angel.

When she spotted the glass slipper from Disney World, Jenna could not hold back her smile. She and Justin had accumulated so many ornaments over the years that their parents limited them to one per vacation, so they fought over which one to buy. That time, Justin gave in. Next to the glass slipper was the chapel at St. Michael's College in Vermont, where her parents went to school and were married twenty-two years ago.

But her favorite, by far, was a glass ornament with a painting of the Swan Boats and the Boston Public Gardens, because it reminded her of one of her favorite days of the year — when her family would play tourist in Boston. The Swan Boats were powered by a person peddling at the back of the boat, and every year Justin boasted that he would one day have that job. With the way things were going with him, it seemed that dream would remain a childhood fantasy.

After looking at each ornament and giving sufficient thought to the memory that accompanied it, Jenna's eyes found their way back to a small gift under the tree, wrapped in different paper from the rest. It was Christmas Eve, late in the evening, and normally Jenna would be eager to open her gifts, hounding her mother until she let her open at least one before bed. But that small gift under the tree made this year different than in past years.

Two short weeks before, Jenna lost a very special person in her life. Agnes was an elderly neighbor whom Jenna had befriended. She was a simple, warm-hearted old woman with more life inside her than could be contained in one soul and a gaze that pierced through to the heart of whatever matter was at hand. She was always tuned in to the needs of others, without letting on how much she suffered in her own body.

Just before Agnes died, as if she had known that she would spend this Christmas in Heaven, she came knocking on Jenna's door with a gift. "There's no need to give this to me now," Jenna protested. "I'll come by on Christmas Day, and we can exchange gifts then." But Agnes insisted, so Jenna gave in and accepted the early present.

When Agnes passed away, Jenna's mother asked her if she would like to open that gift early, but something deep within Jenna's heart told her it was not yet time. It was a mysterious knowledge, not unusual in her relationship with Agnes. Jenna somehow knew she was not yet ready to receive the gift, so there it sat under the tree until Christmas Day.

Jenna picked up Agnes' gift and slowly ran her fingers along the red ribbon that decorated the tiny box. Her thoughts drifted back to the first time she met Agnes.

***

It was sixteen months before, and Jenna and her mother had just moved into their new home, right after her parents divorced. She had just returned from her first visit with her father in his new apartment and was settling in to unpack the endless pile of boxes in her bedroom. Although the room was filled with her furniture, it still felt as though she was in someone else's house.

Her stomach turned at the thought of starting a new school the following week. As she halfheartedly uncovered the boxed items wrapped in old newspaper, she came across a framed photo of herself with her brother taken fourteen years before. Justin was five and Jenna was two. They sat huddled together, too little to fill the oversized gold armchair that sat in the corner of her old living room. That chair — like Justin — hadn't made it to the new house.

After he got involved with a new group of friends in their old neighborhood, things quickly went downhill. The constant fighting between Justin and their parents made home feel like a war zone. Justin's behavior eventually became more than their parents' already strained marriage could bear. When they announced they were getting divorced, and that Jenna, Justin, and their mother would have to move, because they would no longer be able to afford their large home, Justin vanished. It was shortly after his eighteenth birthday.

The doorbell rang, and Jenna jumped up, happy for an opportunity to put off her unpacking. She arrived in the living room to find an elderly woman with a warm smile handing her mother a large serving dish piled high with stuffed shells, meatballs and sausages. The aroma of the steaming hot food filled the room and awakened her appetite.

"Good evening. I'm Agnes from next door," the woman said, gesturing toward the small, yellow cape that sat next to Jenna's grey-blue ranch. "I thought you might be too busy unpacking to cook dinner." With Agnes' presence, the air in the room seemed to grow lighter.

Her mother gratefully accepted the plate. "Thank you. I hadn't realized it was almost dinner time. We were just about to take a break. Can you stay for some tea?"

Agnes glanced at the boxes that lined the living room. "I'd better get home," she said with a wink. "I still have laundry to get done before it gets too late."

Jenna was disappointed when she left so soon, but Agnes made her promise to stop by for a visit once she got settled in. "I've lived here for more than fifty years, so I can tell you anything you'd like to know about the neighborhood."

***

Tears stung Jenna's eyes as she carefully placed the gift back under the tree. She had grown to love Agnes so much in such a short time. One visit had quickly turned into another, until Jenna was spending a good chunk of her free time with Agnes, who happily put aside whatever she was doing when Jenna would visit. She found herself wandering over when things were difficult or when she was down but didn't quite know why. A short visit with Agnes could change her perspective and lift her mood. When she felt herself slipping away, somehow Agnes pulled her back.

If, on the surface, Agnes' age made her seem a bit out of touch at times, Jenna didn't have to probe too deeply to discover that there was a quality about her that made her ageless. She was connected with something far beyond herself. Her eyes seemed to contain the fountain of youth, even if her face and hands revealed the number of years already spent on Earth. At times, during their conversations, Jenna would see things in an altogether different light and would get the distinct sense that she was the one who was out of touch and not Agnes. She didn't know how she was going to get by without Agnes in her life.

It was nearly midnight, but Jenna was still wide awake, because she was on school vacation and had slept late the past few mornings. She had just returned from spending Christmas Eve with her father and his side of the family, and she'd come home with bags full of opened presents. She hadn't eaten much of the elaborate Italian feast that was a Christmas Eve tradition in her family. Her depression over losing Agnes surely contributed to her loss of appetite, but she also sensed there was more to it. Even deeper in her heart than her grief was a feeling of restlessness, a sense that a significant change was beginning to take place inside her, but she was unable to perceive what it could be.

In the time leading up to Christmas, Jenna had been bored. Christmas had always been her favorite time of year — the anticipation of gifts, her family coming together, vacation from school — but this year seemed different. Jenna was becoming aware of a longing for something more meaningful in her life, and she sensed that this had something to do with her friendship with Agnes. It felt as if something in Agnes had rubbed off and begun to work inside her. It was like a spark jumped from Agnes' heart into hers and was moving around within her.

As Jenna sat beneath the Christmas tree, her gaze kept returning to that unopened present from Agnes. As long as it remained unopened, it was somehow as if Agnes were still alive, as if there would be one last conversation, one last precious word from her. Knowing that Christmas Day was almost there, Jenna began to dread opening that gift, and for the first time in her life, she dreaded the arrival of Christmas Day.

Just after this anxious feeling came upon her, peace gently washed over her coming to her like a surprise visit from an old friend. It brought with it a sense of well-being that reminded her of the peace she once knew as a young child, surrounded by a loving family and before turmoil had entered her world. At first, she thought she could feel Agnes present, sitting right next to her. This feeling put her at ease, then faded as she became aware of an even deeper peace.

While Jenna sat resting in this sensation, she saw a bright light next to the Christmas tree, out of which stepped the most exquisite creature she ever saw. He was tall and slender with long wings that ran from well above his head to the base of his back. His white garment had gold trim around the collar and base of the sleeves, and he wore a golden rope tied around his waist. His entire being radiated gentleness, and a soft hue, barely perceptible, surrounded him, giving him a consoling quality.

Although there was a softness about him, his eyes burned with a love that seemed to purify all he looked upon. As she gazed upon the angel, she felt as though she was standing before the most beautiful sunrise. The experience absorbed her whole being.

The burning question in Jenna's heart jumped out from her lips, so that the sound of her own voice took her by surprise. "How are you so beautiful?"

The angel smiled in a way that drew Jenna out of herself, and she could feel her grief melting from her heart. "God made me this beautiful for you."

With those words, she felt love envelop her entire being so profoundly that she did not know if it rose up from within or embraced her from outside, but a feeling deep in her heart told her that she was looking upon her guardian angel.

The angel moved closer with an outstretched hand, carrying a white rosary and offering it to Jenna. It was brighter than any white she had ever seen. He looked expectantly toward Jenna, who sensed he would not proceed until she accepted the rosary.

She hadn't prayed the Rosary since she was a young child, but many times when she would stop in to visit Agnes, her friend would be slowly moving the beads through her fingers, deep in prayer. Although Jenna took it for an old-fashioned habit that she didn't want to waste a precious visit with Agnes asking about, there was one time that she inquired.

Jenna could still see the expression on Agnes' face, as though she longed to share something meaningful and close to her heart. "This prayer is my gateway to Heaven." Jenna often wondered about those words but could never quite figure out what they meant. How could such an apparently monotonous prayer bring Agnes so much joy?

Strengthened by this memory of Agnes, who seemed so close, Jenna took the rosary into her hands. She didn't dare speak, but rather stood watching for what the angel would do next. It was the first time in nearly two weeks that her heart didn't ache from losing Agnes. Jenna felt alive in the angel's presence and every care, every anxiety, melted away. He had come from the place that is the source of every consolation, and Heaven's residue accompanied him. It was as if pain was not permitted into that moment.

"Jenna," the angel said, "Come with me on an adventure through time, and indeed beyond time, into the eternal. We will enter the mysteries that are the source of all life and that possess the power to make your heart whole. In your hands, you hold the key. Let us go together on this unforgettable journey."

CHAPTER TWO

Introductory Prayers

For I know well the plans I have in mind for you, says the Lord, plans for your welfare, not for woe! Plans to give you a future full of hope. When you call me, when you go to pray to me, I will listen to you. When you look for me, you will find me. Yes, when you seek me with all your heart, you will find me with you, says the Lord, and I will change your lot (Jeremiah 29:11-14a).

Jenna looked down at the rosary in her hand, and doubt began to rise within her. The angel's presence had captured her attention, but her intrigue became mixed with disbelief, and she began to feel apprehensive. *What on earth is going on with me?* she wondered. *Maybe I'm losing my mind!*

Before her doubts could settle in, the angel moved toward her, and holding a rosary in his own hand, gently stroked the crucifix. He made the Sign of the Cross and began to pray the Apostle's Creed. *"I believe in God, the Father Almighty, Creator of Heaven and Earth..."*

The words of the prayer made their way into her soul like a beautiful melody, drawing her out of herself and beckoning her on a journey to a far-off place. Their sound was pleasant, and behind the words were strength and authority. Although Jenna hadn't prayed the Creed since she was a little girl, the familiar words brought her comfort, and she instinctively joined the angel in her heart until the prayer seemed to spring up from deep within. She could feel their effect on her as she prayed.

Then came the Lord's Prayer: *"Our Father, Who art in Heaven, hallowed be Thy name; Thy Kingdom come; Thy will be done on Earth as it is in Heaven; Give us this day our daily bread; And forgive us our trespasses as we forgive those who trespass against us; And lead us not into temptation; But deliver us from evil. Amen."*

Then the three Hail Marys and Glory Be followed in the same way. With the Hail Marys, the angel asked for an increase in Jenna's faith, hope, and love. After the Glory Be, the angel, whose eyes were closed, slowly opened them and looked over at Jenna, who found herself deep in the moment.

When the angel made eye contact with Jenna, she felt a quiver in her stomach. His strong, soothing voice and confident eyes, dancing with anticipation, were in stark contrast to the fear and doubt within her. Her world had changed so quickly over the past couple of years. Things she believed to be foundational in her life had disappeared and were replaced by turmoil and uncertainty. She sometimes felt as though she were alone on a tiny raft in the middle of a turbulent ocean.

Part of her wanted to flee in order to protect herself from trusting him and being disappointed, even if he was an angel. She thought of how quickly she had come to depend on Agnes' friendship, and then how painfully fast she lost her.

Being with Agnes had been like standing in the sun on a cold afternoon. Her warm hospitality helped Jenna to relax and let go of whatever was troubling her. She had even begun to wonder if perhaps God had seen her struggling and might be sending some help through Agnes. This brought hope, and that hope had begun to take root in her life. Until, like a bolt of lightning, came that early morning fourteen days ago that reopened the wounds that had been healing in the warm rays of Agnes' love.

A lump formed in Jenna's throat as she recalled being awakened from a deep sleep by the sound of an ambulance, jumping out of bed, and rushing over to a window, where she saw the ambulance pulling up to Agnes' home. She ran next door as fast as her legs would carry her, only to be told that Agnes had passed away in the night. Jenna's heart shattered anew as she remembered the ambulance driving away, taking with it her closest friend in the world. By the time her mother came over, tears running down her face, she was unable to do anything except hold Jenna in her inconsolable grief.

The thought of that morning made Jenna so angry at God that she felt a rage she didn't even know was inside her. If that's what love inevitably came to, she would never bother to love again. And if God gave his gifts only to rip them away, she wanted nothing more to do with him.

Jenna, who had been lost in thought, looked around for the angel and found he had been keeping a respectful distance. Then he came closer. "Some important feelings are rising up in your heart, Jenna. There is a storm raging inside you, but if you come with me, you will soon meet the one who can calm any storm, even the storms that rage within the human heart."

"I doubt God cares about my problems. If he cared about me even a little, he would have protected me from so many things."

When Jenna looked at him for a response, she saw in his eyes her own suffering reflected back as if it were his pain, too. His compassion set her at ease. "God is no stranger to human weakness, and he longs to show you just how close he is, if you will let him." Although part of her still wanted to close her heart and turn away, a hope rose in her that she could not suppress. She knew that this visitation was somehow connected with Agnes and the gift under the Christmas tree, so she resolved to see it through, allowing herself to be carried by a strength that was not her own.

The angel accepted Jenna's reluctant, but sincere, consent to move on. As he looked into her eyes, warmth filled her soul. Taking the lead once again, he promptly announced, with reverence at the very mention of the event, "The first Joyful Mystery is The Annunciation."

The Joyful Mysteries

CHAPTER THREE

The Annunciation

Sing and rejoice, O daughter Zion! See, I am coming to dwell among you, says the Lord (Zechariah 2:14).

The angel began the first decade of the Rosary as Jenna listened silently to the prayers she once knew. She allowed the familiar words of the Our Father to wash over her. Then, the first Hail Mary: *"Hail Mary, full of grace, the Lord is with thee. Blessed art thou among women and blessed is the fruit of thy womb, Jesus. Holy Mary, mother of God, pray for us sinners now and at the hour of our death. Amen."*

All of a sudden, Jenna felt the ground below her shake, and she squeezed her eyes shut. The angel put his hand on her shoulder and held on firmly. Soon, her feet stood on a dirt floor, and, when she opened her eyes and looked around, she realized she was in another place and time.

A few feet away, there was a young woman who looked a little younger than Jenna. At first glance, aside from her striking beauty, she seemed quite ordinary. But there was something about her that attracted Jenna and drew her to observe more closely. She possessed a quiet confidence, which gave her a regal quality that shined through her entire demeanor.

Jenna felt an intrinsic familiarity with her, even an intimate connection, although she was certain she had never met her. The woman was kneading a batch of dough in a large wooden bowl. When she finished, Jenna watched her divide the dough into small cakes. Her mouth moved silently as she worked. While her gaze was fixed on the dough, her thoughts appeared to be far away, as if deep in prayer.

Suddenly, a bright light, emanating from the center of the room, captured the young woman's attention. She stopped working and sat down on a nearby bench. An angel stepped out of the light and came toward the woman. Bowing his head slightly, he said, "Hail Mary, full of grace, the Lord is with you." His words were slow and deliberate, and the joy they contained reverberated through Jenna's whole being as his melodic voice filled the room.

The woman knit her brow in confusion, but the angel reassured her. "Do not be afraid, Mary. You will conceive and bear a son, and you are to name him Jesus. He will be the Son of God, the long-awaited Messiah who will sit on the throne of David his father, and there will be no end to his kingdom."

Mary stepped back, away from the magnificent creature, as if more space would help her absorb the significance of his words. She looked off into the distance for a brief moment, then back toward the angel. She swallowed hard and asked, "But how can this be? I have no relations with a man."

He gazed upon her with great tenderness. "The Holy Spirit will descend upon you, and the power of God will overshadow you. Therefore, the Child conceived will be the Son of God." The woman listened attentively. "And your cousin Elizabeth, who was barren, has also conceived a son in her old age. Nothing will be impossible for God."

Jenna's guardian angel was standing right next to her, looking upon the scene as intently as she was. Without moving an inch, he whispered, "The salvation of mankind is hanging upon her response. Heaven and Earth are awaiting her 'Yes.'"

Then he turned slightly toward Jenna. "Her assent to God's plan would put her in grave danger. Since she is betrothed to Joseph, being with child would be considered adultery, which is punishable by stoning."

Jenna wasn't sure what to make of that. It certainly seemed like God allowed a lot of unnecessary suffering in people's lives. "Why would God put her in such a difficult situation?" she asked. "Why does he have to make it so difficult for Mary to do what he is asking?"

"It is the difficulty of the situation that reveals the depths of Mary's faith," he replied. "Her trust is what makes her response so powerful." She couldn't argue with that, but it still felt unsettling.

Jenna had mixed feelings about faith. She sometimes met people who seemed to use God or religion as a neat and tidy way to avoid dealing with life's difficulties and thinking for themselves, and she wanted no part of that. She knew Agnes' faith was tried and true, but just because faith worked for Agnes didn't mean it had to be Jenna's path. There were times when she wasn't even sure if she believed God existed.

Jenna had never had any trouble speaking openly with Agnes about these things. Agnes' faith ran deep, and she didn't take offense at Jenna's questions and doubts the way some people did. One particular conversation with Agnes burned brightly in her memory.

***

"Agnes, you have to admit that the world is full of chaos," Jenna said. "Half the families I know are falling apart; school can be a scary place; and terror recently struck our own city. Besides, all my prayers for my brother and my parents' marriage have gone unanswered. If God does exist, he always seems silent when I need him most."

"It certainly can appear that way, can't it?" Agnes replied.

Jenna looked down and nodded. "Whenever I watch the news, it just depresses me. All the heartache only proves that God isn't interested in our struggles. If God is so loving, why does he seem so distant? If he is so powerful, why doesn't he ever intervene in the important matters that plague our world? And if he isn't interested in these larger things, he can't possibly be interested in my problems." Jenna peered into Agnes' eyes as if she could find her answers there if she only looked hard enough. They were filled with compassion, but not despair.

"I don't pretend to understand God's timing or his ways, Jenna. But I am certain of one thing: the same faithful God with whom I have fallen ever more deeply in love throughout my life will, in his perfect time and in his perfect way, respond to the longings of your heart. Deep in my spirit I can feel your time approaching, Jenna. I just don't know from which side of Heaven I will witness it."

***

Jenna took a deep breath and returned her attention to Mary. She knew what Mary's response would be, but she found herself listening as if she had never heard the story. "I am the servant of the Lord," Mary said, with a profound bow. "Let it be done to me as you have said." With her assent, the Angel Gabriel departed.

"Although there were many details that Mary did not yet know," Jenna's angel said, "she trusted in God's plan and in his providence. Her response would echo back to the beginning of time and soar into the future, flowing forth from time into eternity and back through time, never losing its power or impact throughout the ages.

"Mary was the first to believe, the first Christian, and her 'Yes' would be a striking example for all generations. Never has one word from any creature contained so much power. At Mary's 'Yes,' came the meeting of Heaven and Earth, and in an instant, centuries of preparation and prophecy were realized. God entered completely and irreversibly into human history, sharing man's lot from the moment of conception, his most vulnerable moment."

It seemed odd to Jenna that something so important happened in such an uneventful way. Granted, an angel appeared to Mary — that was extraordinary — but now that she thought about it, why wasn't the whole event more dramatic, perhaps in a more public place with smoke and trumpets so that everyone would believe? Jenna wondered aloud why God was so discreet and so allusive, both here at the Annunciation and in her own life.

Her questioning gaze settled on her angel, who was still looking directly at her. "Jenna, even the angels are astonished at the humility of God and the dignity of the human destiny." Then he took a step closer and gently touched her arm. "Remember Mary's 'Yes.' You will later see its full cost." A chill ran through Jenna's body, for she knew the sorrowful events to which the angel was referring.

Shaking her head to regain her composure, Jenna said, "I still don't see what any of this has to do with me." She didn't understand the purpose of this journey, and her own troubles — one big one in particular — weighed heavily upon her heart. What would become of Justin?

Jenna really missed having her big brother in her life. Justin always knew just how to cheer her up. Sometimes he would take her to hang out in their tree house or to a nearby park to shoot hoops, where it was always easier for her to unload her problems. But in the months before he disappeared, he had become a different person. Jenna cringed as she remembered the day she realized just how serious the problem had become.

***

"Put that back right now, Justin," Jenna screamed. "Has it really come to this? You've resorted to stealing from Mom to buy your drugs?"

Justin grabbed Jenna's arm digging his thumb into her bicep. Her knees buckled at the sharp pain. "Don't worry about it," he said, releasing her arm. "It's just a loan. I'm going to pay her back." But she knew that wouldn't happen. She no longer believed anything he said.

Taking a step back, out of his reach, Jenna said, "I'm so tired of your lies. You used to protect me. Now you terrify me." She looked in his eyes, hoping to see some semblance of remorse, but she only saw annoyance. As she ran out of the room, the turmoil of the past few months began to settle into her soul.

***

With renewed determination, Jenna said to the angel, "What I really want to know is why I lost Agnes when I needed her most. I want my family to be back together and my brother to be safe. No offense, but I don't need to be taken through some glorified religion class." She didn't want to seem ungrateful, but she thought if she could somehow get the angel to understand her frustration, perhaps it would move him to action. After all, if he could bring her to this place, maybe he also had the power to do something about her problems.

"Bear with me, Jenna," he replied. "The answers you are looking for do not come quickly or easily. But I can promise you this. If you enter these mysteries with an open heart, you will see God's response to your suffering and just how very personal it is."

It wasn't exactly what Jenna wanted to hear, but at least his promise brought a little hope. She knew she could turn away from this experience, but she didn't really have anything to turn to. Then she remembered something Justin used to say: "Go big or go home." She might as well stick it out. Besides, that's what Agnes would have wanted.

The angel stood silently next to her, as if waiting for the struggle inside her to subside. After a few minutes, he prayed the Glory Be. *"Glory be to the Father, and to the Son, and to the Holy Spirit as it was in the beginning is now and ever shall be world without end. Amen."* Then he pressed on.

"To truly pray the Rosary, Jenna, is to live its mysteries, to breathe them in until they become part of you. As you meditate upon these events, allow their wisdom to guide you and draw from them the graces contained in each one. As you make them your own, their power will enter your life.

"Never be afraid of asking God for too much, because his infinite love can never be exhausted. God has an amazing plan for your life, too, Jenna, as he did for

Mary's. There is a mission that is only yours. Learn from Mary the joy of saying 'yes' to God's plan."

Jenna still had a hard time believing the angel's words. *Was it God's will that I end up alone in a new school without my brother and my family broken apart? Where was God's plan in all that chaos?*

Then Jenna thought of how many times life must have appeared pretty chaotic to Agnes. Yet, like Mary, she chose to trust that God would bring her through her difficulties. Agnes used to say that God didn't bring her around her problems, but instead he brought her through them.

She had nothing to lose by trying, so she obeyed the angel's request. As Jenna offered her first prayer, she felt like a little girl kneeling beside her bed. *"God, if you have a plan for my life, a mission just for me, help me to believe that you are real and help me to say 'yes' to that plan with a trust like Mary's."*

The angel glanced up toward Heaven. "Jenna, your request is rising like incense to the throne of God." Then he lowered his gaze and paused reverently before announcing, "The second Joyful Mystery is The Visitation."

CHAPTER FOUR

The Visitation

They transported the ark of God on a new cart and took it away from the house of Abinadab on the hill. Uzzah and Ahio, sons of Abinadab, were guiding the cart, with Ahio walking before it, while David and all the house of Israel danced before the LORD with all their might, with singing, and with lyres, harps, tambourines, sistrums, and cymbals (2 Samuel 6:3-5).

Jenna and the angel continued on in the same manner as before. The angel prayed aloud while Jenna followed along silently, allowing the rhythm of the prayers to calm her, like the steady sound of waves crashing on the beach. Then she returned her focus to the scene unfolding before her as the angel informed her that it was now a couple of days after the Annunciation had taken place.

She wondered how Mary could possibly resume everyday life after such an experience. What would she do next? Would she go to Joseph and try to explain?

Would she go into hiding to protect herself and her unborn Child from potential danger? Would she seek counsel from a rabbi to better understand what had happened? Even with so many unknowns, Jenna could see no fear on Mary's face. Only serenity.

Jenna watched as Mary conversed with relatives. They were asking her to reconsider a journey she was preparing to make, but Mary insisted she must go. After embracing her, they provided her with several containers and flasks. "Where is she going?" Jenna asked the angel. It seemed strange that Mary would choose to travel at a time like this.

"Remember, Jenna, Mary learned from the Angel Gabriel that Elizabeth, a much older woman, was six months along in her pregnancy. In those days they didn't have grocery stores or washing machines, and, as you can imagine, ordinary daily tasks took a lot of effort. So, out of concern for her elder cousin, Mary quickly embarked on the nearly one hundred-mile journey to the home of Elizabeth and her husband, Zechariah, to be of assistance in any way she could."

While the angel spoke, Jenna examined him as if she were seeing him for the first time. As he illuminated the mysteries of the Gospel, a gentle light emanated from his eyes, and his calming presence helped Jenna relax and focus. As they delved deeper into the mysteries they were witnessing, his white garment grew even brighter, and he became more animated.

Jenna's angel again placed his hand on her shoulder, and she instinctively closed her eyes.

***

Before long, they were standing outside a small, stone house, high upon a hill, watching Mary approach in the distance. There were terraced hillsides and valleys as far as she could see. A soft, fresh breeze brushed back the hair from Jenna's face as she took in the breathtaking view. Vibrant red, yellow, and white wildflowers dotted the spring landscape.

Mary's pace quickened as she approached her cousin's home. While they waited, the angel moved closer to offer some insight.

"Mary's compassion for Elizabeth in her time of need brought her to the one person with whom she could contemplate the events taking place in their lives. Although their circumstances were shrouded in mystery, Mary knew Elizabeth was somehow connected with what was unfolding in her own life."

Jenna knew the importance of having someone in your life who understood you. Agnes had been that kind of friend. Whenever they would talk, she always seemed to grasp far more than Jenna could express. She recalled an afternoon when, anxious about the possibility of losing Justin forever, Jenna went to visit Agnes.

***

Agnes was sipping tea in her favorite armchair while Jenna sat on the floor by the fireplace with a mug of hot chocolate, worrying about what would become of her brother.

Agnes sighed and nervously shifted in her chair. "This is still difficult to talk about, Jenna, even after all these years." Taking a deep breath, Agnes continued, "When I was about your age, my brother went off to fight in World War II and never returned. To this day he is still classified as Missing in Action."

"War can come in many forms," Agnes said, her eyes full of compassion. "For some it is violence at school or at home, while others battle addiction or the addiction of a loved one, and for some it can come in the form of a broken family. Although their battles may look different, every war leaves its victims disillusioned, grieving and robbed of their ability to trust." Although Agnes could not solve her problem, she had felt a little better just knowing that someone understood how much she missed her brother.

***

As she watched Mary and Elizabeth, it occurred to her that perhaps it was God all along who was behind her friendship with Agnes, just as he had orchestrated the visit between Mary and Elizabeth when they needed each other most.

When Mary reached her cousin, the two shared a knowing glance and then embraced. Although Mary had no way of sending word that she was coming, her elder cousin seemed to be expecting her. Elizabeth said, "Blessed are you among women, and blessed is the fruit of your womb. And how fortunate am I that the mother of my Lord should visit me? The moment I heard your voice, the Child in my womb leaped for joy."

Mary responded, "My whole being proclaims the greatness of the Lord, and my spirit rejoices in God my savior. He has looked favorably upon his lowly servant, and now, every generation will call me blessed. The Lord has come to help Israel, remembering the promise of mercy he made to our fathers, to Abraham and his descendants."

Jenna was intrigued by these two women. If God really sent his Son into the world, he had placed these women at the forefront of the most significant event in history. Yet on the surface, it just looked like an ordinary visit between two cousins.

"It's strange that such an important event happened in such a simple way," she said. "To look at them from a distance, you'd never know all that was happening beneath the surface."

The angel nodded in agreement. "Yet this was God's plan. He wanted Jesus' first months to be spent in the company of two faithful women whose mutual esteem and affection would fill his early days with peace and joy. If you pay attention to this scene, Jenna, you can learn something important about the heart of God. He prefers to dwell among faith and charity rather than riches and fanfare."

This reminded Jenna of something Agnes once said, which she shared with the angel. "Many search for God in dramatic events, but he is more often veiled in simplicity and humility."

The angel smiled. "The prophets had their information and their role, but God's plan would first unfold amid the intimate friendship of these two faith-filled cousins."

The scene came to a close while the angel prayed the final Hail Mary of the decade of the Rosary that they had been praying. As she listened to the prayer, Jenna suddenly noticed that most of the words of the Hail Mary were from the Angel Gabriel's greeting at the Annunciation and from Elizabeth's greeting at the Visitation. They were starting to come alive.

The angel prayed the Glory Be, then asked with the gentle prodding of a good teacher, "What graces would you like to ask God for from this mystery?"

Jenna didn't have to think too long. There was something about the profoundly simple faith of these women that intrigued her. Perhaps it was because something about them reminded her of Agnes. *"Lord, if this is real, help me to recognize your presence in the simple encounters of everyday life and to know the faith and joy that these women share."*

The angel bowed his head and waited for a moment, as if allowing time for Jenna's prayer to reach Heaven. Then he announced the next mystery. 'The third Joyful Mystery is The Nativity of the Lord."

CHAPTER FIVE

The Nativity

In the beginning was the Word,
and the Word was with God,
and the Word was God.
He was in the beginning with God.
All things came to be through him,
and without him nothing came to be...

...And the Word became flesh
and made his dwelling among us,
and we saw his glory,
the glory as of the Father's only Son,
full of grace and truth
(John 1:1-3a, 14).

Jenna and the angel pressed on. Although many questions still turned in her head, Jenna was eager to visit the Nativity scene. Not only was Christmas her favorite holiday, but tonight she was also in the midst of its celebration and could feel a tangible connection to it.

With all the loss she had recently experienced — her parents' divorce, Justin's disappearance, and Agnes' death — Christmas just wasn't the same this year. She had lost the excitement of exchanging gifts, and the holiday just reminded her of everyone she missed. Her heart ached to see Justin again, and she wondered if her brother was thinking about her and missing the Christmas traditions they once shared. A smile made its way onto Jenna's face as she recalled Christmas morning four years ago.

***

Jenna woke up early and wandered into the living room, thinking she was the first one up. To her surprise, Justin came bounding through the front door. His face dropped when he saw Jenna.

"Where were you?" Jenna asked. She knew something must be up.

Justin looked pleased when, before he could answer, their parents were on their way down the corridor from their bedroom into the living room. *No fair, that's just his luck.*

Her father threw in a Frank Sinatra Christmas CD while her mother doled out the gifts. "This one is from Mom and Dad to Jenna. This one is from Justin to Mom.

Oh, and look," she said, feigning surprise as she handed a box to Justin. "This one is from Santa."

In between opening gifts, Jenna tried to make eye contact with Justin, but with the fine-tuned skill of an older brother who wished to keep a secret, he avoided her stare. After the Christmas morning frenzy, they only had a little time to get ready before aunts, uncles, cousins and friends descended upon the house for Christmas dinner.

Later that night, pretending to hug Justin good night, Jenna whispered playfully into his ear, "You know I'll figure it out sooner or later, so you might as well tell me."

He shot her an impish smile that seemed to say, "Not this time, little sister."

The next evening, she sat waiting for him in the living room with a look of victory when he returned home for dinner.

"Hey Justin, I saw the strangest thing today."

"Oh yeah?"

"Yeah. I went past the Bakers' house this afternoon and the kids were playing with a bunch of new toys — Joey had a bike, Ryan had a scooter, and Richie was breaking in a new baseball glove. Some pretty cool stuff."

"Well, yesterday *was* Christmas. What's so strange about that?" His eyes sparkled as he tried to hold back a smile, and Jenna knew she had him.

"Well, Mr. Baker passed away this year, and Mrs. Baker just lost her job. I wonder how she could afford such expensive gifts." Then she added, "By the way, Justin, what did you ever do with that all that money you earned over the summer mowing lawns? You were going to upgrade all your ski equipment, but ski season is here, and you still have those old skis in the garage."

Justin looked at the floor and blushed. "Okay, Okay! You're not mad that I kept it a secret, are you?" They usually didn't keep secrets like that from each other. "I didn't know if Mrs. Baker would accept the gifts, so I wanted to keep it on the down low."

"I'm not mad, but I would have loved to have helped you pick out the toys!"

"Next time," he said, still smiling.

Jenna jumped up and threw her arms around his shoulders. He blushed and tried to brush her off, as if she were making too big a deal out of it, but Jenna held on for a few more seconds. She never knew what to expect with Justin, but that was one of the things she loved most about being his sister.

***

Perhaps that is why it took me so long to figure out when he was in trouble, she thought, as the angel prayed the Our Father. *He was always up to something, so it wasn't obvious at first that this last time he was up to no good.*

When he prayed the first Hail Mary, the angel placed his hand on Jenna's shoulder, and she slowly closed her eyes. When she opened them, he informed her she was in Joseph's home, and he proceeded to catch her up to speed. "When Mary returned to Nazareth from her visit with Elizabeth, she was well into her fourth month, and before long, it would be evident that she was with child. However, she determined to say nothing to Joseph and to trust that God would work out the details of this plan he had already set irreversibly in motion. So she trusted and waited in prayer and silence.

"When Joseph learned that his betrothed was with child," he continued, "he was confused and hurt, but he did not want to expose her to shame and the penalty of the law. He decided to divorce her discreetly since, according to Jewish law, betrothal was as binding as marriage. But God intervened by sending an angel to him in a dream, who said, 'Joseph, do not be afraid to take Mary into your home. She has not been unfaithful; this Child has been conceived through the Holy Spirit. He is the Messiah, and you are to name him Jesus.'

"So in an act of tremendous faith and humility, Joseph did as the angel said. Together they awaited the birth of Jesus in great joy and anticipation, sharing the weight of the responsibility of their role in God's mysterious plan." Jenna hadn't quite remembered all the details of the story, so she enjoyed hearing the angel recount it.

She watched Mary, nearing the end of her pregnancy, and Joseph prepare for a journey. As quickly as she was able, Mary gathered together enough food to last a few days. She filled a container with what looked to Jenna like pita bread. She packed almonds, figs, and other dried fruit into another basket, and in a third she carefully placed olives, goat cheese, and eggs. There was also a small jar of honey and several skins of water. Jenna observed a concerned, pensive expression on Joseph's face as he fed and watered his donkey.

"They must be getting ready to go to Bethlehem," Jenna said, fascinated as she watched the preparations.

"Yes, you might remember they are going in obedience to a decree issued by the Roman emperor requiring them to be enrolled in a census."

Jenna's eyes grew wide as she wondered how Mary could possibly make the arduous trip so late in her pregnancy. "It can't be that safe for Mary to travel in her condition. Can't they be excused under the circumstances and stay home?"

"If only it were that easy, Jenna. They lived in a world where violence and extortion were the norm. Soldiers terrorized their people every day, squeezing every dime they could from even the most poor. To disobey could have meant death. Besides, they knew God could easily step in at any moment to change their circumstances if he saw fit, so they trusted that there was a purpose for their journey."

Then he added, "Sometimes God's ways are hard to understand at first." Jenna wondered if he was referring to her own circumstances.

She shot a quick glance at the angel, then looked back at the scene. "You're saying that sometimes God's ways only make sense in hindsight, when you understand the big picture?"

The angel nodded. "And sometimes they don't fully make sense until Heaven," he said with a slight smile. "Knowing this can spare a lot of anxiety and frustration." Jenna still thought that God could have made things easier, for Mary and Joseph, and for herself. After all, he *was* God.

***

While they were in Bethlehem, Mary went into labor. There were so many travelers in town for the census that, by the time they arrived, there was no room left at the only inn in the area, so Jesus' birth had to take place in a stable.

"Mary and Joseph had provided other means for the birth of Jesus," the angel said. "They wanted it to be at home, in comfort and provision, surrounded by loved ones, and they were deeply pained to see it come about while they were away. But God had other plans for the birth of his Son."

As the angel spoke, Jenna's eyes were glued to the stable. She took in everything as though she were learning about it for the first time. She had seen so many replicas of this stable that she was desensitized to its reality. The sight of a manger always brought memories of Christmases spent with family and close friends, sharing an abundance of food, gifts, and laughter. It made her feel happy and safe. But here she only saw poverty. It was cold, and the Holy Family had to rely on heat from donkeys and oxen to keep warm. The air was dusty, and the sounds and smells of the animals filled the stable. Jenna's heart sank.

She tore her eyes from the scene before her and looked directly at the angel. "This night is not at all how I imagined it," she said.

"Nobody would have imagined the birth of the Messiah in this way," he replied. "The King of kings was not born into a palace, and there were none of the comforts of even the humblest of homes. The manger was indeed a place of intense joy and fulfilled promises, but at the same time its poverty and obscurity called forth profound faith."

Jenna reflected on Mary and Joseph's life together so far. An angel had appeared to each of them to reveal God's plan — to Mary at the Annunciation and to Joseph in a dream. But these revelations brought more questions than answers. Mary and Joseph had to have wondered why Jesus was born into such a violent time. Why would he live his life in the midst of such an oppressive military regime, where his message was less likely to be accepted? Why did he come into such poverty? And Jenna knew that the challenges surrounding his birth would be nothing compared to what was to come at the end of his life.

"I was hoping you might help me by taking away my problems, but you can't do that, can you?" she asked the angel, suddenly feeling small.

"Jenna, you are the only one who can walk your path. Just as Mary and Joseph had to walk by faith, you, too, have to learn to trust God in the midst your own struggles and uncertainties." Her heart grew heavy upon hearing the angel's words. It seemed like an impossible task. Even if he were right, you can't just manufacture faith.

Trusting anyone, especially God, had become more and more of a struggle in recent years. Why would God, who could stop anything, allow the things she loved and needed most to be taken from her?

Jenna recalled a time when she was feeling low and asked Agnes this very question. To Jenna's surprise, instead of giving an answer, she told Jenna about the days when, after losing her husband to cancer, she learned to depend on God for everything. "Sometimes help came in the form of a generous person or an unexpected opportunity," Agnes had confided. "But ultimately it was through the love and dreams I held for my children that God gave me the strength to go on. I worked in restaurants and factories, cleaned homes and offices, and did whatever it took to make ends meet."

Jenna wasn't sure if it was Divine Providence or sheer stubbornness that got Agnes through those long years when she struggled to raise her four young children alone. But there was one thing she did know. When Agnes talked about God, she was talking about an intimate friend who never failed her, even if at times he appeared to be distant.

Jenna longed to know the peace that Agnes' faith brought her. But just the thought of not knowing where her brother was, or the nagging loneliness she often battled, brought a tidal wave of fear that washed away any faith she may have possessed.

Jenna turned her attention back toward the stable, where Joseph prepared the manger to receive the baby. The immense joy on his face became overshadowed by a disheartened expression. "Why does he look so sad?" she wondered aloud.

The angel looked compassionately at Joseph. "The cradle he had lovingly and meticulously constructed with his own hands had to be left behind. In this place he could offer no cradle, no crib, only the simplest of beds." Jenna had never thought of that, but it made sense that being a carpenter, Joseph would have made nothing but the best things for Jesus.

She watched as Mary placed Jesus, all bundled up, on a bed of hay in a manger, the feeding trough for animals. Then her gaze was drawn to the sky above the stable, where she could see the Star of Bethlehem burning brightly, almost dancing, as though it could not contain its joy. She had been standing at enough of a distance to take in the whole scene, but suddenly she felt a strong desire to approach the manger. She looked over at her angel, who appeared to understand her desire. He went over before her and made a pile of hay for her to kneel upon.

As she knelt down, he asked softly, "Do you see why our Lord chose to come into the world in this way? Against this backdrop of poverty, his love shines more brightly." Then he reverently stepped back and gave Jenna a moment alone in the Divine presence.

As Jenna knelt before the manger, a tangible peace came upon her. She looked down at Jesus' face which, young as he was, radiated an intense love that gently penetrated her heart. Then she looked at his body, carefully and lovingly wrapped to protect him from the cold. Here, God was approachable. He was so small and so vulnerable that it was impossible to be afraid of him. His weakness was utterly disarming. *Perhaps that is why he came to the world in this way. After all, who could refuse to receive a baby?*

For the first time since she could remember, Jenna felt that God was truly with her. There in that manger, he was dependent, so much in need of love. God now had a human heart. If God had gone to such lengths to be that close to her, perhaps the things she was anxious about in her own life would somehow turn out okay. And if God was with her, he must also be with Justin, even in his darkest moments. Jenna felt a glimmer of hope.

After some time, she sensed the angel was waiting to take her somewhere, so she stood up and followed along. The air felt heavy, and they were moving slowly. It was as if God's grace was draped over her shoulders like a shawl. The stillness and quiet of the scene permeated her spirit. She knew she was walking on holy ground.

The two slowly made their way to a field some distance from the stable, where there were shepherds guarding their flocks. As the shepherds kept watch, staff and rod in hand, Heaven gently broke through the profound stillness that covered the night and a gentle, peaceful light shone all around them.

The shepherds looked up from their task to see that an angel had appeared. Their faces grew pale and they clutched their staffs, but the angel reassured them. "Do not be afraid, I come to you with wonderful news. Today, in the city of David, the Messiah and Lord has been born.

He is wrapped in swaddling clothes and lying in a manger. Go to him!" Then, suddenly, with the angel, Jenna could see countless other angels. Their joyful singing filled the air and they praised God saying, "Glory to God in the highest and on Earth peace to people of good will."

The shepherds left immediately to head to the manger, and Jenna and her guardian angel followed behind them. Their walk turned into a jog as they struggled to keep up with the shepherds. When they arrived, the shepherds prostrated themselves before the Baby. Then they stood up and told Mary and Joseph all that had happened to them. They left talking with excitement about the wonders of God and what would become of this Baby.

The angel stood next to Jenna as she rested in the power that filled that holy night. As she gazed off into the distance, contemplating what she had witnessed, she felt as though she were in a dream. However, the sight of the bright star, the smell of the animals, and the cold air against her skin were far too vivid for a dream.

***

Jenna looked toward the night sky, and three men on camels came forth from the horizon. As she watched them make their way to the stable, she realized they were the three wise men. They greeted the Holy Family and presented their gifts of gold, frankincense, and myrrh.

Mary and Joseph's eyes were wide as they received the gifts on Jesus' behalf.

"Can you imagine what Mary and Joseph must have thought when, soon after his birth, three kings arrived from so far away to pay homage to Jesus?" the angel said, pulling Jenna from her thoughts. "The Magi presented gold, a gift for a king; incense, a gift for a priest; and myrrh, expensive embalming oil, which brought a foreshadowing of Jesus' death to the joy of his birth. They found Jesus by reading the stars, and when they departed, they would never be the same again. God's plan and revelation were already so far reaching.

"Jenna, always follow your star, even when you cannot see where it is taking you," the angel continued. "When you follow the light that God provides and persevere in trust, this is when miracles happen." She again felt hope and promise, even though her own problems seemed insurmountable.

After praying the Glory Be, Jenna didn't yet want to leave the peace of the stable, so she hesitated when the angel made a gesture to move on. But he insisted they continue.

"There's so much more that awaits us, Jenna. For what grace would you like to ask God from this mystery?"

Overwhelmed by all she had just witnessed, she didn't know where to start, until her angel reassured her. "You are not leaving forever. If you choose, you can return to these places time and time again through prayer, whenever you desire. For now, simply ask God for what it is you need today, in the present moment."

Although she was still struggling to accept what she was witnessing, her doubt was gradually giving way to intrigue and hope. Perhaps there was more to the faith of her childhood than she previously thought. She determined that, although she still didn't understand what this was all about, she would see this journey through and try to be open, especially because she knew Agnes would want it that way. So she prayed, "*Jesus, you chose to be born into poverty more than two thousand years ago. My life feels poor and stark at times. But I see that poverty does not scare you; it seems to attract you. If you truly do exist, come into my heart this Christmas, the way you came into that stable.*"

Eager to continue on, the angel announced, "The fourth Joyful Mystery is The Presentation of Jesus in the Temple."

CHAPTER SIX

The Presentation of Jesus in the Temple

When the LORD, your God, has brought you into the land of the Canaanites, just as he swore to you and your ancestors, and gives it to you, you will dedicate to the LORD every newborn that opens the womb; and every firstborn male of your animals will belong to the LORD (Exodus 13:11-12).

O ur Father, Who art in Heaven...
By now Jenna pretty much knew the words to the prayers and was able to say them along with the angel. As the angel placed his hand on Jenna's shoulder, she closed her eyes and allowed the Our Father to carry her into the next scene, while the Hail Marys drew her more deeply into contemplation. She was entering into the rhythm of the Rosary.

When she opened her eyes, Jenna was standing at the bottom of a gigantic staircase outside a colossal stone structure. The sheer majesty of the building revealed that she was somewhere of monumental significance. Off in the distance she could see the Holy Family approaching.

The angel set the scene, helping her to understand the context of a tradition so foreign to her own culture. "As faithful Jews, Mary and Joseph fulfilled every detail of the Law of Moses. A woman was considered ritually unclean for forty days after the birth of a son, after which she had to be purified. She could offer a lamb and a pigeon or turtle dove, or if she could not afford a lamb, she could offer two pigeons or two turtle doves," he explained. "When the time for Mary's purification had come, Mary and Joseph journeyed to the Temple in Jerusalem to offer the prescribed sacrifices.

"In addition to Mary's purification, Jesus, as their firstborn son, would be presented to God, as is also prescribed in Jewish law. In this way, the Author of the law submitted himself to its precepts."

Jenna watched Mary tenderly carry Jesus toward the Temple, pressing him close to her body and shielding him from the dust that rose up from the road. Joseph carried a cage containing two young pigeons. "They could not afford a lamb, but they brought to the Temple the Lamb that would later be sacrificed for the whole world," the angel said, calling Jenna's attention to the irony of the situation.

When the Holy Family arrived at the Temple, Jenna and the angel walked beside them as they climbed the staircase. Upon entering a courtyard, they encountered a man praying with his hands raised gently toward Heaven. "This is Simeon," the angel said, looking at the man with great tenderness. "Like so many throughout Israel's history, he is a true man of God, waiting for the fulfillment of God's promises to his people. The Holy Spirit had shown him that, before his death, he would hold Israel's long-awaited Messiah."

When Simeon laid eyes on the Baby Jesus, a look of recognition spread across his face. He joyfully approached the Holy Family as if he had been expecting them. He carefully took the Baby into his arms, as though receiving a precious treasure, and tears streamed down his weathered face. Looking toward Heaven, he said, "Master, now I can die in peace, knowing that I have seen your salvation, the glory of Israel and a light for the whole world."

He blessed Joseph and Mary. Then a look of profound compassion came upon his face as he looked into Mary's eyes and said, "Your Son is destined for the fall and rise of many in Israel. He will be sign from God that many will oppose. And a sword will pierce your own heart, too, so that the inner thoughts of many will be revealed."

Simeon's words, intimately connecting Mary to Christ's Passion and humankind's redemption, left a lump in Jenna's throat as she thought about the form that sword would take. Even in those early days of Jesus' life, the Cross seemed to loom on the horizon. Jenna tried to push it out of her mind, but the theme kept returning. It made her think about how she was in the midst of the most difficult time in her life when she met Agnes. It seemed as though with God, joy and suffering were often mysteriously intertwined.

Through the people she was encountering in these mysteries, Jenna was beginning to see faith in a new light. Having faith didn't mean that everything would always be easy, but it was more like trusting that God was at work even when we don't understand. It was choosing to focus, not on circumstances, but on the One who is greater than all circumstances. Jenna knew she was a long way from that kind of faith, and she wondered if she would ever have it. *How would I even go about trying to get it?*

Her thoughts were interrupted when she saw an old woman walk toward the Holy Family. The woman's frame was thin and her face wrinkled, but a deep confidence shined in her eyes. "This is Anna," the angel said. "She is a widow who was married for only seven years when she was young and had no children. Like Simeon, she spent all her time in the Temple praying and fasting."

With a warm voice, Anna greeted the Holy Family, then looked toward Heaven and thanked God for what she was witnessing. "For the remainder of her years, she would tirelessly speak about this Child to all who were awaiting the Messiah," the angel said.

Jenna took a deep breath. She had seen so much in a brief time, and she was trying to wrap her mind around it. She had heard these stories as a young child in religious education or when she would occasionally go to church with her family. But she was seeing them through different eyes now. She wasn't sure if it was because of her friendship with Agnes or because of the place where she was in her own life. Maybe it was a little of both.

She thought back on what she had seen so far. God had worked through the faith of so many trusting souls to bring about these miracles. He worked most beautifully through Mary, who gave her wholehearted "Yes" to God's plan; through Joseph and his heroic trust; through Elizabeth, Zechariah and the unborn John the Baptist, who leapt in his mother's womb at Mary's greeting; God chose the poor shepherds working in the field to meet his newborn Son; he drew the three wise kings, who discerned his presence through reading the stars; and now, he revealed his Son to the prophets Simeon and Anna, who had been wholeheartedly awaiting the arrival of the Messiah. Jenna couldn't help but recall what Agnes had once said to her. "God clothes himself in simplicity and wraps the extraordinary in the ordinary."

In fact, there was something about Simeon and Anna that reminded Jenna of Agnes. Through these two prophets Jenna caught a glimpse of the power of Agnes' seemingly ordinary life of prayer, faithfulness, and love. Jenna remembered how Agnes always seemed connected to something beyond herself, and now she was beginning to understand.

Mary and Joseph started to leave the Temple area and Jenna followed. When they reached the staircase leading out of the Temple, the angel touched her arm as a signal that she should not follow.

"Can't we go with them?" Jenna asked.

"Our journey through Jesus' infancy ends here," he replied. "After Mary and Joseph had fulfilled the requirements of the Law, they returned to Nazareth. Jesus would grow up in the love and intimacy of family life, which is so sacred to God that he went to extraordinary means to ensure that his Son did not go without it. The next mystery will take us into his childhood."

They prayed Glory Be, and the angel asked what grace she would like to pray for through this mystery.

"I pray to be more like Simeon, Anna, and the others I have encountered so far through these mysteries, so that I might recognize God in the seemingly ordinary events of life, and

for faith so that I can learn to trust him even when he seems far away."

The angel paused reverently for a moment. Then he turned her attention to the next mystery. "The fifth Joyful Mystery is The Finding of the Child Jesus in the Temple."

CHAPTER SEVEN

The Finding of Jesus in the Temple

After three days they found him in the temple, sitting in the midst of the teachers, listening to them and asking them questions, and all who heard him were astounded at his understanding and his answers (Luke 2:46-47).

As they began the prayers of the last Joyful Mystery, Jenna was still standing at the top of the staircase at the ancient Temple in Jerusalem. Her angel, ever by her side, informed her that twelve years had passed since the Presentation.

From Jenna's vantage point she could see multitudes of people making their way toward the Temple, traveling in large groups. Tents dotted the surrounding hills and sounds of singing, tambourines, and laughter hung in the air. The angel gently placed one hand on her arm while gesturing with the other toward one of the groups of pilgrims. Jenna immediately recognized Mary and Joseph, although she did not yet see Jesus.

"It was Passover and, as was their custom, the Holy Family traveled from Nazareth up to Jerusalem with many relatives and neighbors to celebrate the Feast," the angel explained. "The population of Jerusalem swelled with the great numbers that came from near and far each year to commemorate this defining event in the history of the Jewish people."

When he finished speaking, the angel placed his hand on Jenna's shoulder and she closed her eyes.

***

When she opened them, they were walking toward one of the Temple courts, where she had met Simeon and Anna in the previous mystery. Her angel set the scene while they walked. He explained that it was the custom of the Holy Family to celebrate Passover in Jerusalem but this particular year, after the feast, the caravan with which Jesus was traveling left while he remained behind for three days.

When they reached the Temple court, Jenna stopped suddenly as she spotted Jesus, now twelve years old, sitting in the midst of some learned looking men and asking them questions. She immediately recognized the scene.

Being the only story in the gospels of Jesus as a boy, it was often read during her religious education classes.

Although Jesus was younger than Jenna, he somehow seemed older. She thought it must be partly due to the responsibilities a boy his age would have had in his time, but it also seemed to go beyond that. He seemed to carry a weight on his shoulders that was uncharacteristic of a twelve-year-old, but not easily perceptible because he maintained the lighthearted attitude of a child. His size and features made it evident that he was still a boy, but his demeanor made him appear more mature.

Since they were so close in age, Jenna felt an immediate connection with Jesus. As she observed him, it occurred to her that Jesus, too, experienced the joys and struggles of growing up. Jesus was at the age where he would have discovered that life, as beautiful as it was, also had its share of suffering and brokenness. By now, he would have known disappointment and the pain of losing loved ones.

Living under Roman oppression, Jesus would have witnessed the brutality of the Roman soldiers. He would have tasted fear and faced his own limitations. She could easily imagine Jesus struggling to make sense of the injustices and poverty around him.

She thought about some of her experiences over the past few years — Justin's disappearance, her parents' divorce, moving and changing schools, and then, just as she was beginning to adjust, losing Agnes. Jenna somehow felt less alone knowing that Jesus, too, walked some difficult roads throughout his life and that the world was not always as he would have wanted it to be.

She also reflected upon Jesus' future and the degree to which he would later experience pain and abandonment. It was in these early years that he must have developed the self-mastery he would need to respond with love and forgiveness.

Although she had encountered Jesus as a Baby in the manger, his humanity now seemed even more accessible. She felt as though it would be the most natural thing in the world to walk up to him, take his hand, and talk to him about everything. And he would understand like nobody else.

Glancing over at her angel who stood close by, head slightly bowed and hands folded, Jenna wondered if he was praying for her while she encountered the Child Jesus. Then she turned her focus back to the scene before her.

Jesus' conversation with the elders was outside of Jenna's earshot, but their expressions spoke volumes. Jesus sat straight, shoulders relaxed, looking as though he were in his element. His eyes danced as he smiled softly from time to time. The elders leaned in closely as Jesus spoke, occasionally glancing at one another with their mouths open and nodding. From their wide-eyed expressions, she would have thought they were speaking with a renowned teacher. It looked to Jenna as though he possessed a key that was opening for them a treasure chest revealing riches they didn't know existed.

As she watched Jesus with the teachers, she was intrigued to see, once again, that youth was no obstacle for God. Earlier she had seen the Incarnation take place through the cooperation of a young virgin, and then she saw John's witness from the womb. At the manger she experienced the love of God through the Baby Jesus, and now the wisdom of a twelve-year-old was confounding the great sages.

She then thought of Simeon and Anna, and of course Agnes, and she concluded that we have something unique to offer at every moment in our lives. It is never too early or too late. We are never too weak or too poor. This knowledge gave Jenna a sense of purpose and meaning as she suddenly became aware of a power within that she never knew was there.

Her thoughts were interrupted when she saw Mary and Joseph return to the Temple with anxious footsteps and dark circles under their eyes, as if they hadn't slept for a while. Jenna remembered from the story that they had been searching for Jesus for three days. When they finally found him safe and unharmed, Joseph looked up toward Heaven and breathed a sigh of relief, while Mary ran toward Jesus.

Jenna understood their fear all too well. Seeing their concern reminded her of the days following Justin's disappearance — the fear, the panic, and then the disbelief when they discovered his letter. "I've decided to move out on my own. Don't worry about me. I'll be in touch when I get settled." But he never was in touch.

She remembered those dark circles under her mother's eyes, too, and the sleepless nights wondering if he was okay, if she would ever see him again. At first, Jenna expected him to return home at any moment. *Surely, he will come to his senses. He must know how worried we are.* But as time passed, her hope faded and she just prayed he was still alive. On Mary's face she could see her own mother's pain.

Joseph caught up with Mary, and they approached Jesus together. Then Mary asked, "Son, why did you do this to us? Your father and I have been anxiously searching for you."

"Why were you searching for me?" Jesus replied. "Didn't you know that I must be in my Father's house?" Mary looked at Joseph with furrowed brows, but Joseph remained silent, gazing thoughtfully at Jesus. Then Jesus rejoined his parents, and Jenna watched as they departed Jerusalem together.

"The years to follow would be quite ordinary," the angel said. "Jesus would continue to grow as a devout Jew and a loyal son. He would perfect the trade he was learning from Joseph, assisting him, and eventually providing for himself and his mother after Joseph would pass away."

As the Joyful Mysteries came to a close, Jenna took a moment to catch her breath. She walked toward the immense staircase that led down from the Temple courts and sat down on one of the steps to rest. The angel followed and sat next to her, looking at her with great hope. "Can you feel what is happening, Jenna?" he asked. "The first five mysteries of the Rosary, the Joyful Mysteries, are having their effect. They are opening your eyes to the closeness of God and drawing you into his saving plan for a broken world and for your own life." Jenna looked down. She wondered if he was right. Something was definitely happening inside her, although she still wasn't sure what that was.

They prayed the Glory Be, and the angel waited in silence for her to formulate the prayer that would bring the Joyful Mysteries to a close. After a few minutes, she prayed. *"Jesus, I am beginning to see that you are with me, even when I can't see you. You experienced life's joys and difficulties and go before me in all things. Please help me to see that you are near, even when I cannot understand your ways."*

Then the angel announced, "The first Luminous Mystery is The Baptism of Jesus."

The Luminous Mysteries

CHAPTER EIGHT

The Baptism of Jesus

Now there was a Pharisee named Nicodemus, a ruler of the Jews. He came to Jesus at night and said to him, 'Rabbi, we know that you are a teacher who has come from God, for no one can do these signs that you are doing unless God is with him.' Jesus answered and said to him, 'Amen, amen, I say to you, no one can see the kingdom of God without being born from above.' Nicodemus said to him, 'How can a person once grown old be born again? Surely he cannot reenter his mother's womb and be born again, can he?' Jesus answered, 'Amen, amen, I say to you, no one can enter the kingdom of God without being born of water and Spirit (John 3:1-5).

Jenna looked over at her guardian angel and thought about how attentive her companion was proving to be.

He seemed to sense when she needed explanation or encouragement and when she needed space. The safety she felt in his presence caused her to experience a freedom she hadn't known since the carefree days of her early childhood. It was as though time had stopped and she could fully enter into each moment as it unfolded before her, seeing with more clarity the whirlwind of emotion swirling around within. Her struggles and doubts still remained, but she was beginning to see things with new light.

Jenna was gradually discovering that there was more to the faith of her childhood than she previously thought. The peace she remembered feeling as a young child was slowly returning, trickling back into her soul as she came to realize that God was, indeed, present in so many places where she previously thought he was absent. Although there was still a long way to go on this journey, Jenna was discovering some hope in the midst of uncertainty, a hope that encouraged her to press on.

As they began the prayers of the first decade, the angel placed his hand on Jenna's shoulder, and she closed her eyes. Suddenly she felt dirt beneath her feet and heard a man's voice crying, "Turn away from your sins! The Kingdom of God is near." She opened her eyes to see a rugged-looking man addressing a vast crowd. His hair was long and unruly, and his clothing was made from animal skins. The man seemed possessed by a sense of urgency as he tried to impress upon his listeners the importance of turning away from what was wrong and back toward God.

Although the preacher attracted many people, he did not mince words. "Do not be complacent. It is not enough to have Abraham as your father. If you do not leave behind your sins and produce good works to prove you have repented, you have no place in God's Kingdom."

This man is obviously not concerned with popularity, Jenna thought. At first she wondered why he was being so harsh. *What could these people have done?* But when she observed him more closely, she saw in his demeanor a profound humility. He didn't seem to be taking pleasure in his task, but there was deep concern in his voice. It was as if he were trying to prepare them for something, something big. Then, suddenly, it occurred to her that she must be looking upon John the Baptist, Jesus' cousin.

About thirty years had passed since she first encountered him in the womb of Elizabeth at the Visitation. She remembered how he leaped in his mother's womb at the sound of Mary's greeting. She thought of the events surrounding his conception — how the angel told Mary that Elizabeth, although older, was expecting a baby, and how Mary had gone immediately to her cousin as soon as she heard the news. Even then, his destiny seemed intertwined with that of Jesus.

The angel stood near Jenna as she continued to observe John. While he preached, he was also baptizing in the river those who came forward and expressed a desire to turn away from their sins.

"John's mission was to prepare the way for the Messiah," the angel explained. "Jesus was about to begin his public ministry, and as long as people remained attached to unhealthy behaviors, they would be unable to wholeheartedly embrace his teaching.

"Some were on dangerous paths, and his firmness was for their benefit. Others needed to be shaken out of their complacency and inspired toward deeper levels of faith and love of neighbor. Like today, many people believed they were basically living good lives, but Jesus would soon stretch their standards with the love he would model from the Cross. He would show the world that love was not about being a nice person when it's convenient, but it meant putting others first, even at great personal cost.

"Like men and women of every age, pride and greed, infidelity and dishonesty, lust and selfishness, along with so many other sins embedded in the human experience, threatened to keep their hearts from Jesus' message. John's baptism in the Jordan River would help them face their weaknesses and understand their need for a savior. It was John's task to face them with a decisive moment."

Jenna listened as John instructed people on how to live well. "If you have extra clothes, share with a person who does not have enough, and if you have enough food, do likewise."

To tax collectors he said, "Stop collecting more than what is due and keeping it for yourself."

And to soldiers, he warned, "Do not abuse your power or falsely accuse anyone, and instead be content with your wages."

One man, his gaze shifting between the ground and John, looked as if he were working up the courage to speak. When it was his turn to be baptized, he asked in a loud voice, "Are you the awaited Messiah?"

"I am baptizing you with water," John replied, "but another is coming who will baptize you with the Holy Spirit and fire. I am not worthy to loosen the straps of his sandals."

One after another, she watched John immerse the people into the river. As they came up from the waters, shoulders relaxed and joy radiating from their faces, Jenna couldn't help but wonder what John would have said to her if she had come to be baptized. What would she need to change in order to prepare herself to meet Christ?

A memory from the day Justin disappeared flashed into her mind. Jenna had come home from school to find her mother sitting alone and crying. Rather than comforting her, she lashed out and blamed her for Justin and her father leaving. Jenna could still see the shattered look on her mother's face as she turned and ran to her room.

It occurred to Jenna that, in some ways, her behavior wasn't completely different from that of the soldiers and tax collectors, who in their selfishness took shortcuts to make their own lives a little easier, no matter how it hurt others.

Although Jenna had not run away like Justin, she knew she fled in her own way when she closed her heart and withdrew from those who loved her. In her pain she even turned from God, because he wasn't intervening the way she wanted. She wanted him to make her problems go away, and when he didn't, she acted more like a spoiled child who assumed her parents didn't love her, because they didn't let her do whatever pleased her, or made everyone else behave as she wanted. She had eventually apologized to her mother for the way she had acted the day Justin left, but her guilt still felt heavy. *Perhaps it's because I never made peace with God.*

Jenna's thoughts were pulled from her meditation when she spotted Jesus coming toward John to be baptized. As soon as she saw him, she somehow knew who he was. All her attention was fixed on Jesus as he made his way toward his cousin. Jenna looked in his eyes and saw love burning like a gentle fire. There was a sense of deep purpose in his movement, and he possessed a purity that permeated his whole being. While there was an innocence about him, there was also understanding and compassion in his gaze.

When Jesus reached the place where John was baptizing, John protested, saying that it was Jesus who should be baptizing him. But at Jesus' urging, he relented.

As Jesus came up from the waters, Jenna saw the sky open, and what appeared to be a dove swept down upon him and hovered for a moment before disappearing back into the sky. Her angel whispered that it was the Holy Spirit coming in the form of a dove. Then a voice came down from the heavens: "You are my Son whom I love. With you I am well-pleased."

Jenna felt a surge of power run through her as the heavens opened and she witnessed the revelation of Jesus' identity and of God's presence: Father, Son, and Holy Spirit.

Jenna's angel remained close by. After a few minutes, he said with amazement lingering in his voice, "It was, of course, not necessary for Jesus to be baptized, because he never sinned. But it was out of love that he entered the waters of baptism. He allowed himself to be counted among sinners, anticipating his own baptism that would come in the form of his Passion and Death. Jenna, Jesus goes before you in more ways than you could ever know."

As the scene came to a close, Jenna's thoughts wandered to her own Baptism. Sometimes when she would flip through her baby album, she would see pictures of herself with her family and the priest in front of the baptismal font. Jenna had always thought of her Baptism as an occasion for her family to have a party and to celebrate her life. She had never thought much about its spiritual significance.

"I remember that day," her angel said, his eyes gleaming with joy. Jenna smiled as she realized that he would have been there, too. "When you were baptized into the family of God, your soul was forever changed. The grace that you received is always with you, Jenna, whether you choose to live by it or not. At any time, you can reawaken that dormant grace and unleash its power in your life. Can you imagine the extraordinary change that would come upon the world if every Christian did just that?

"Their relationship with God would be limitless as they drew ever closer to him in faith, hope, and love. Recognizing God's Spirit living in every soul, people would treat one another with reverence and respect, and so much pain would be avoided."

Jenna's angel paused, and the two stood gazing down the river, while Jenna tried to let all she had witnessed sink in. After some time, her angel's expression grew more serious. Appearing deep in thought, he said, "Jenna, if you decide to live as a Christian, you can expect that it will sometimes require heroic courage to be faithful, and it will often feel like you are swimming against the tide. There are many dangerous influences that permeate the culture in which you are immersed. Every day, unhealthy images stream into people's homes through various media, pulling their minds and hearts away from what is good and healthy.

Then there is the powerful industry that grows rich treating people as mere objects for pleasure and exploiting God's sacred gift of sexuality by treating it as a commodity to be bought and sold, leaving boys with unrealistic expectations and robbing them of self-control, while leaving girls to feel they need to compete with airbrushed images if they are ever to be loved and desired."

His voice trembled as he talked about the lucrative industry that exists to destroy innocent life during its most vulnerable stages, leaving so many women feeling shattered from a decision made, not in freedom, but under pressure and false promises, often feeling as though they never had a real choice.

"Then there are the advertisements that play on girls' insecurities, subtly telling them they are not beautiful enough to be wholly and completely loved by another, all to turn a quick profit. Such a climate chips away at young peoples' sense of self-worth, causing them to forget that, created in the image and likeness of God, they are made for greatness. Jenna, if you are to persevere, you will have to hold fast to Jesus," he said, almost pleading.

"However, God can never be outdone in generosity. The grace given to you at your Baptism provides concrete help to recognize and do what is right and to resist what is harmful. The challenges and pitfalls are real, Jenna, but grace is real too," he assured her. "And when you fall, you can always confess your sins and get right back up."

Jenna stood on the banks of the Jordan River reflecting on the angel's words. Although she knew that she didn't completely grasp everything he was telling her, her trust in God's providence was growing. There was so much that was still a mystery, but Jenna felt increasingly grateful for the opportunity to take another look at the faith she had — perhaps prematurely — cast aside.

As the scene before her came to a close, Jenna watched Jesus depart from the river and head towards the desert. He left behind him much discussion and speculation by those who had witnessed that great event.

After Jesus left, Jenna bowed her head and joined the angel in praying the Glory Be. Then she formulated her prayer to conclude the first Luminous Mystery. *"Lord, help me to take to heart John the Baptist's words and turn away from the things in my life that pull me away from being the person you intended me to be. Please help me to grow in the grace given to me at my Baptism, and to understand that you go before me in all things, especially when I'm feeling afraid and alone."*

Then the angel announced, "The second Luminous Mystery is The Miracle at Cana."

CHAPTER NINE

The Miracle at Cana

His mother said to the servers, 'Do whatever he tells you'
(John 2:5).

They prayed the Our Father, and the angel placed his hand on Jenna's shoulder. When she opened her eyes, she was no longer at the Jordan River, but in a village looking out onto a joyful celebration. The sun was shining brightly, and the atmosphere was lighthearted. Jenna immediately felt happy to be there.

The conversations around her were filled with hope and anticipation, and everybody seemed delighted to be part of such a joyous occasion. There was an abundance of food and laughter, and the wine was flowing. As Jenna wandered around among the groups of people with her faithful companion by her side, he told her they were at a wedding feast in the village of Cana.

As she took in the sights and sounds of the ancient, yet timeless, ritual, her angel explained that in Jesus' culture, weddings took place over seven days, and people would come at various points throughout the week to celebrate with the couple. Jenna watched joyfully as guests greeted old and new friends and expressed their happiness for the couple. She almost felt as though she were an invited guest at the party. She wished her own family could be with her, because she knew how delighted they would be at seeing such a gathering.

As the wedding guests interacted, Jenna noticed how, without the distractions of modern technology, or the rush to move on to the next activity or appointment, people seemed more absorbed in one another's company. They possessed a sense of connectedness that Jenna sometimes longed for in her own culture.

As she wandered around, Jenna spotted the bride and groom mingling with a group of wedding guests and made her way towards them. She wondered what life held in store for them. *Would he be good to her? Would he be faithful in both the big and the small ways?* She also wondered what life had in store for herself. *Would she get married one day? What would her husband be like? How many children would they have?* She knew from watching her parents how hard it can be to depend on another, to trust a person with your future and your heart. The pain that comes when happily ever after falls apart still felt raw in

Jenna's heart. She surprised herself when she said a silent prayer for the happiness of the bride and groom. It was the first time since she could remember that she prayed without being prompted.

After some time, she noticed out of the corner of her eye that Jesus was present in one of the groups, talking with his mother. The sight of the two of them standing together stopped Jenna in her tracks. Nearly twenty years had passed since she last saw them together in the Temple at Passover. She was struck by the physical resemblance between them until she remembered how Jesus received his entire humanity from his mother. It made sense that the resemblance would be striking. Since Jesus was born when Mary was quite young by modern standards, Jenna was also surprised to see how close in age they were. It almost looked to Jenna as though Jesus could be her younger brother, except for the fact that they clearly related to one another as mother and son.

Jenna drew closer to listen to their conversation. "The bride and groom have run out of wine." She could hear the compassion in Mary's voice. The angel explained that having no more wine to offer guests would be humiliating for the newly married couple.

"How does your concern affect me?" Jesus replied. "My time has not yet come."

Mary turned to the servers with a serene smile and said, "Do whatever he tells you."

Jesus looked down for a moment, and then his loving gaze returned to his mother. "Fill these jars with water," he said to the servers, gently holding eye contact with Mary, while motioning toward six large jugs.

When the servers filled the jugs to the brim, Jesus said, "Now take some to the headwaiter."

After the waiter tasted what was in the jars, he called over the bridegroom. "Why have you kept the best wine until now? You are supposed to serve the best wine first and the inferior wine after the guests have had their fill."

Jenna could only imagine the embarrassment the couple would have endured had the wine run dry and their wedding ended prematurely. She was touched that Mary made their concern her own and used her influence to help the couple. And Jesus, for his part, did not just help them out enough to get them out of a jam. He provided nothing but the best for his friends.

"In her great love and compassion, Mary perceives your needs even before you do, as she did with the couple, and brings them to Jesus who responds with abundance," the angel said, his love and esteem for the Queen of Angels pouring forth from his voice. "Like every good mother, Mary longs for the well-being of her children, and just as at Cana, she did not hesitate to bring the couple's need to her Son, she will do the same for you. To a mother, every need and desire of her child is important."

Jenna's thoughts drifted to her own situation. If it were true that Jesus could turn water into wine, then he could change anything. Yet as compassionate as he was, he had not yet changed her circumstances. Perhaps by praying for God to fix all her problems, she was presenting Jesus with the wrong water. *Perhaps I should try a different approach. Maybe the water Jesus wants to start with is my heart, not my circumstances.*

She could still pray for Justin's safety and recovery, but maybe she needed to give God some space to work by trusting him. Rather than becoming more bitter each day Justin didn't return and telling God how to handle the situation, she might simply pray that, in God's time and way, he would bring peace to her family.

After all, without that change of heart that John preached about, she would be stagnant. Agnes used to say that God specialized in bringing good out of bad when we let him, but trusting anyone to do that, including God, was more easily said than done. Jenna hoped she would be able to make that leap of faith one day soon.

Jenna stood amidst the joyful celebration, which went on uninterrupted. Once again, Jesus seemed approachable, not distant. He did not keep himself aloof but was fully involved in the joys and difficulties of everyday life.

As Jenna glanced one final time at the wedding feast, her angel told her it was time to move on. So she bowed her head, and they prayed the Glory Be. Then she said, *"Lord, help me to trust that you truly do care about all my needs, even if at times they seem insignificant in the grand scheme of things. I pray to always trust that you know the best solution to every difficulty and that you always act in a way that is for my ultimate good and the good of the others involved. May I also learn to lean on Mary's prayers and trust that she sees my needs even before I do."*

When Jenna finished praying, her angel thanked God for all the graces received so far and asked that she would be granted even more light to understand those that still lay ahead. Then he announced, "The third Luminous Mystery is The Proclamation of the Kingdom."

CHAPTER TEN

The Proclamation of the Kingdom

The Spirit of the Lord is upon me,
because he has anointed me
to bring glad tidings to the poor.
He has sent me to proclaim liberty to captives
and recovery of sight to the blind,
to let the oppressed go free,
and to proclaim a year acceptable to the Lord
(Luke 4: 18-21).

When the angel announced this mystery, Jenna felt a surge of anticipation, realizing she would soon be with the first disciples as Jesus taught about the Kingdom of God. She remembered hearing the gospel stories as a child and being perplexed as she tried to unlock their meaning. She was hoping that they would make more sense now that she was a little more mature and had some context — and of course the aid of her trusted companion.

Soon they were standing by the shores of a large body of water, which her angel informed her was the Sea of Galilee. The feel of the sand beneath her feet and the clean, fresh air heightened her senses. The hills in the distance and the lack of salty air gave it a different feel from the New England beaches she was used to, but simply being by the water energized her. The beach was one of her favorite places to think.

As they continued praying, Jenna saw Jesus walking by the sea, looking on as two fishermen were casting a net into the waters. "That's Simon, whom Jesus would later rename Peter, and his brother Andrew," the angel said, gesturing toward the men.

Jesus called out to them, "Follow me and I will make you fishers of men." They stared intently at Jesus and, for a moment, the intensity in the air was palpable. Then, to Jenna's surprise, they dropped everything and went with him.

Jesus, Peter, and Andrew walked further along the seashore toward two young men mending their nets with an older man, whom Jenna assumed was their father. She learned from the angel that they were James and John. Jesus called them, too, and they immediately left their boats and their father, and followed him. Jenna was puzzled at how the first disciples could leave everything so quickly to respond to Jesus' call.

"This was not the first time these men had encountered Jesus," her angel clarified. "They heard him teach on other occasions and saw him perform miracles. His words were already at work deep inside, awakening in them a desire for the mission to which he was calling them.

"Here on the seashore they faced a decisive moment, the kind that comes for each Christian in every age. Whether raised in a family where faith is central, or one where it takes a back seat to the rest of life, each person comes to a moment of decision when he must choose whether he will take that leap and follow Jesus. It is, of course, a commitment that is renewed every day and deepens with each passing year, but there are, nevertheless, moments of decision for everyone."

Jenna understood well what her angel was telling her. There were times throughout this journey when she felt as if grace were welling up inside her and stirring in her heart. She knew she would soon have to decide if she would take Jesus' hand and make that jump.

"Like the first disciples, you don't have to understand everything," the angel said. "There will be plenty of time to learn and grow. But the time is approaching when you will have to decide whether you trust Jesus enough to follow him into the unknown." The angel's words roused

Jenna's innate love of adventure, yet at the same time caused her stomach to do somersaults. She was glad she didn't have to make the choice right at that moment. She still needed time.

Before they left the seashore, the angel explained that eight others were also chosen to be Jesus' closest companions, and they would be with him constantly over the next three years. All but one, who would later betray him, would become the first leaders of his Church. Jesus would gradually reveal himself to them, and, over time, draw them more deeply into the mystery of his identity and mission. In addition to the Twelve, many others would follow him.

***

Jenna's guardian angel put his hand on her shoulder, signaling that he wished to take her to a new scene, and she closed her eyes. When she opened them, she was in the midst of a vast crowd gathered along a hillside, the Sea of Galilee now their backdrop. Jesus stood at the top of the hill gazing out upon the multitude. It seemed to Jenna that he was looking into each person's soul. His dark eyes were intense and probing, but there was no judgment in his expression, only love and compassion.

Many present had heard about Jesus and were eager to encounter him firsthand, while others had already begun to follow him closely, the angel told her. Jenna watched as Jesus laid hands on the stream of people approaching him, some with hope in their eyes, others with desperation. Jenna noticed a blind woman in line, lovingly assisted by two friends. All three were full of confidence, practically dancing, as they approached Jesus, as if they had no doubt she would be healed. Jesus cupped the back of her head with one hand and placed the other over her eyes. When he removed his hands, her eyes flew wide open in amazement. "God desired that his Son's radiant smile would be the first thing this woman ever saw," the angel said.

Then she caught sight of a middle-aged man who didn't appear to be sick or injured, but he walked with bent shoulders and heavy steps. Looking at the man with tenderness, the angel explained that he had been orphaned, then abused as a young child and had carried inside him his whole life the pain, fear, and feeling of worthlessness that come from such treatment. Jesus put both arms around the man's shoulders and whispered into his ear for several minutes as tears streamed down the man's face. Then Jesus embraced him, and he left walking proud.

Jenna watched as every person who came to Jesus that day was healed, their faces radiating joy and wonder, and their bodies relaxed as heavy burdens were lifted. She felt a stirring within her own heart as she witnessed the healing and freedom that Jesus imparted.

After some time, Jesus sat down, facing the vast crowd, and began to teach. "Blessed are you if you are poor in spirit, if you know that God loved you into being and his grace alone holds you in existence. Happy are you if you trust God even when life's circumstances tell you not to. If you know that you were made for God alone and that the deepest desires of your heart can be fulfilled only in his love, then the Kingdom of Heaven is already within you.

"Blessed are you if you mourn, if the things that break the heart of your heavenly Father also break your own heart. Pain, division, suffering and death come from sin, which was never God's desire. If you long to let go of your own sin and for your Father to hold you in his arms and heal all your wounds, then you will be comforted.

"Blessed are you if you are meek, if you are you are able to exercise power and authority with self-control rather than self-interest. If you always put first the good of those entrusted to your care, you will inherit the Earth.

"Blessed are you if you desire what is right and just, if you love God's will above your own. This desire comes from God, and with it, the grace to persevere. If you hold fast to this grace, you will be a light showing a weary world the way to God's Kingdom.

"Blessed are you if you are merciful because your heavenly Father will in turn show you mercy. As you forgive and love with a generous heart, the Father will bless you beyond your wildest imaginings.

"Blessed are you if your heart is pure and clean. Happy are you if you turn away from sin, from everything that causes you to fall short of your glorious destiny, of the Father's eternal plan for your life. You will see God everywhere.

"Blessed are you if you are a peacemaker, if you build bridges rather than hold grudges. Happy are you if you see the best in people because God's love will flow from you and you will be called a child of God.

"Blessed are you if you live in this way and still are persecuted. If you live according to my teaching you will be ridiculed, misunderstood, lied about and worse. You may even be killed by those dominated by sin and hatred. But blessed are you if persecution comes your way because yours is the Kingdom of Heaven."

As he spoke, a heavy silence descended from the hill and settled upon the people. Jenna felt as though Jesus was speaking to her alone. His words burrowed their way into her heart like seeds taking root deep within. Jesus was more than a powerful speaker. His words contained an authority her soul had never felt.

She slowly scanned the crowd and looked into the eyes of those around her. Although Jesus' paradoxical teaching was difficult to understand, she could see by their pensive expressions that his words touched them deeply. Many appeared puzzled, and Jenna shared their struggle to understand these challenging words. His teaching seemed to require looking at the world in a completely different way. While conventional wisdom says, "Watch out for Number One and avoid pain at all cost," Jesus was proposing another way. But how could mourning and meekness lead to happiness? What did it look like to be poor in spirit?

As Jenna reflected, Agnes' face popped into her mind. Since the first time they met, Jenna knew there was something different about her, a quality that ran deeper than her warmth and hospitality. Agnes possessed a joy that remained with her, even when she talked about the most difficult times in her life. It wasn't that she didn't suffer. When Agnes would recount the story of her brother disappearing during World War II, her shoulders stiffened as her pain resurfaced. When she talked about her deceased husband, her smile would fade as she wondered aloud what her life might have been like if he had not died so young. And as she recounted stories of raising her children alone, struggling to put food on the table and oil in the furnace, Jenna could see her relive the fear that her children might go to bed hungry or cold. Yet Agnes never lost her peace.

Jenna recalled a conversation they once shared.

***

One fall afternoon, as Jenna sat gazing out the bay window in Agnes' living room at the trees ablaze with the colors of the season, Jenna asked how she could talk about the most difficult times in her life with no trace of bitterness or self-pity. The melancholy feel of autumn had put Jenna in a particularly thoughtful mood.

"I had my moments, believe me, Jenna," she said. "But the tragedies in my life also brought blessings, because they made me realize how much I needed God's grace each day just to make it through. God has a beautiful way of bringing good out of the worst circumstances. I learned first-hand that I could do nothing without God, and my faith grew."

***

Was that what Jesus meant by poverty of spirit? Jenna glanced toward her angel in hopes that he might shed some further light on the mystery.

"In this teaching, called the beatitudes, Jesus proposes a way of thinking that goes beyond a set of rules," the angel said. "He calls his disciples toward a spirit of self-emptying modeled after the interior life of the Holy Trinity. As you imitate it, you participate in God's very nature and share in his own joy. Jesus is teaching his disciples that you cannot acquire true happiness on your own. Like life itself, it is a gift from God."

His tone became more serious. "This means saying 'no' to certain behaviors, Jenna, and turning away from selfish actions that ultimately bring pain, even if they initially bring relief or gratification. Your heart was made to love God and receive his immense love, and his ways alone lead to lasting happiness."

Jenna returned her focus to Jesus, who was still preaching from the top of the hill. He was challenging the crowd to love one another the way God loves. "There is nothing special about being kind to those who are kind to you. Anybody can do that. But if you want to be true children of your heavenly Father, then love your enemies and pray for those who would do you harm."

"This does not mean you should give people license to walk all over you or repeatedly hurt you," her angel clarified. "God wants you to respect yourself. But when someone betrays you, you can offer forgiveness and pray that he will find the happiness that God desires for him. This is the sweetest of victories."

As Jenna thought about whom she might need to forgive, she was surprised that it was Justin who came to mind. She was so afraid of losing her brother that she sometimes forgot she was also angry with him. She missed Justin, but she did not miss the person he had become. At times she was furious at him for causing so much damage and leaving her alone to deal with the consequences. She vividly recalled the heaviness in her chest when she would hear her mother cry herself to sleep, and she couldn't bear that deflated and helpless look in her father's eyes when they talked about Justin. She needed to find a way to forgive him for causing such pain in their family, even if he wasn't around to accept her forgiveness.

Before moving on to the next scene, the angel painted a picture of the rest of Jesus' public ministry. He informed her that for the next three years, Jesus would continue proclaiming the Kingdom of God, and his disciples would remain by his side. Over time, he would gradually reveal his identity and his mission to them. He would spend a lot of time with those who were far from God, because they needed him most. "On one occasion," the angel told her, "Jesus said, 'Those who are healthy do not need a physician, but the sick do." Jenna took comfort in those words, hoping Justin, too, would somehow receive the healing he needed.

"By knowing Jesus," the angel continued, "his disciples came to know the Father's love for them. He taught that each and every person has infinite value in God's eyes, no matter what mistakes he may have made, and that nobody could fathom the lengths to he would go to for each one. Along with Jesus' words came healings, and the disciples saw firsthand his power over nature, evil, and even death. But as time went on, Jesus began to hint more and more of his impending Passion and Death. His disciples did not yet comprehend what would inevitably take place."

Her angel also told her that, although many followed Jesus, there were some who struggled to accept the Kingdom that he proclaimed. "Living under Roman control, they hoped the promised Messiah would free them from the political oppression that was woven into the fabric of their daily lives." Although Jenna didn't live under political oppression, the struggle of these people struck a chord in her. Deep down, she, too, wanted Jesus to free her from her own difficulties, and she still struggled to understand his ways.

Jenna asked the angel if she could hear more of Jesus' preaching, but he replied, "Jenna, these stories are there for you to take up and read anytime you wish. Tonight you are being shown a glimpse of what they contain, but if you persevere in faith, their inexhaustible treasures will be opened for you. However, before we move on to the next mystery, there is one more place I wish to take you." Jenna nodded in consent.

***

The angel placed his hand gently on Jenna's shoulder, and, when she opened her eyes, she was surprised to be standing beneath a large mountain with a massive rock formation. The angel informed her that they were in Caesarea Philippi, a place of pagan worship.

A short distance away, Jesus sat with the Twelve, facing the rock. Her guardian angel brought her closer to the scene, so that she could hear what was taking place. The disciples fidgeted in their seats and nervously looked around. Jenna understood their uneasiness. There was something unsettling about that place.

Jesus had an expression on his face that seemed almost playful as he asked his disciples, "Who do people say that I am?"

They replied, "Some of them say you are John the Baptist, others Elijah or Jeremiah or one of the prophets." Their eyes darted nervously between Jesus and that giant rock formation where false gods were worshiped.

Then Jesus' expression turned more solemn. He looked intently at his closest confidants and asked, "Who do you say that I am?"

Jenna looked at each of the apostles, wondering who would be the first to respond. Then Simon Peter, looking intently at Jesus, replied, "You are the Messiah, the Son of God."

Jesus' eyes widened. "Simon, the only way you could know this is if my heavenly Father revealed it to you. Therefore, from now on, you are Peter, and upon this rock I will build my Church, and the gates of Hell will never conquer it. But for now you must keep this to yourselves and tell no one that I am the Messiah."

The questions that Jesus had just posed to his disciples echoed in Jenna's mind. She thought about the first question, "Who do people say that I am?" Even today, many still believe that Jesus was only a prophet or a great teacher. Yet here in this place, she heard Jesus affirm Peter's declaration that he was, indeed, the Son of God, so much more than even the greatest of teachers. Since a good teacher would never teach something false about himself, Jesus was either "the Messiah, the Son of God," or a really bad teacher.

Jenna then thought carefully about Jesus' second question, "Who do you say that I am?" Jenna did not want to render her own personal response too hastily, because she knew that, depending upon how she answered, a lot could change. She decided she would keep Jesus' question in the back of her mind as the rest of the mysteries unfolded, until she felt better prepared to give a full and honest reply.

While Jenna reflected, the angel had stepped back, giving her some time alone with her thoughts. After a while, sensing he had something to add to her understanding of the scene, Jenna looked toward him and awaited his guidance.

"Here, in seed form Jesus gave some visible structure to his future Church and entrusted it with his own authority," he said, hoping to impress upon her the significance of what she had just witnessed. "Seeing that the Father had granted Peter knowledge of his identity, Jesus bestowed on him a new name and, with it, a particular role and authority that set him apart from the other apostles.

"This office did not die with Peter," he continued. "It is passed down through the generations to Peter's successors, the popes. This is one way that Jesus ensures that the living body of his teaching will never be lost and his followers will never be abandoned.

"There are, of course, risks on Jesus' part to such an approach, but in this way, for better or worse, Jesus could forever share with his Bride, the Church, not only his heart but his mind, as well."

After they prayed the Glory Be, the angel informed her that, from this point on, Jesus would begin to prepare his disciples for the suffering and glorification he was to undergo in Jerusalem.

Jenna was beginning to feel a bit anxious as she thought about the suffering that Jesus would soon endure. Before she had too much time to dwell on it, the angel glanced over at her as a signal to bring the mystery to a close.

So Jenna bowed her head and prayed, *"Lord, help me to truly understand and to live the things you taught. Your ways are so different from my own. Help me to embrace your teaching, so that my true treasure will be in Heaven, where there is real peace and happiness."*

Then the angel announced, "The fourth Luminous Mystery is The Transfiguration."

CHAPTER ELEVEN

The Transfiguration

Beloved: We did not follow cleverly devised myths when we made known to you the power and coming of our Lord Jesus Christ, but we had been eyewitnesses of his majesty. For he received honor and glory from God the Father when that unique declaration came to him from the majestic glory, 'This is my Son, my beloved, with whom I am well pleased.' We ourselves heard this voice come from heaven while we were with him on the holy mountain (2 Peter 1:16-18).

Jenna and her angel began the prayers that would carry them into the next mystery. After so many repetitions, the Our Fathers and Hail Marys were beginning to feel natural, and their increasing familiarity was helping her focus on the mysteries at hand.

Feeling her angel's hand upon her shoulder, Jenna closed her eyes. She soon found herself standing on top of a steep hill looking out over a vast expanse. While she took in the majestic views before her, the angel leaned in and whispered that they were atop Mount Tabor, the Mountain of Transfiguration.

Realizing what she was about to witness, Jenna turned her full attention toward Jesus, a few yards away, absorbed in prayer. She was struck by the fact that, even more beautiful than the spectacular view from the summit of the mountain, was the sight of the Lord in prayer. He sat on a rock, arms outstretched, with his gaze turned toward Heaven. His body appeared completely relaxed as he rested in intimate communion with his Father. Jenna wondered how he could appear calm and refreshed, knowing his Passion and Death were not far off.

As Jenna continued to observe, Jesus stood up, as if someone had asked him to stand, and extended his arms toward the heavens. His face suddenly changed in appearance and his clothes became the brightest white she had ever seen. Then she noticed two men standing next to Jesus and speaking with him. The angel revealed that they were Moses and Elijah, and they were talking about the sorrowful events that awaited Jesus in Jerusalem.

Jenna asked the angel why Moses and Elijah had suddenly appeared on the scene. It seemed strange that these two ancient prophets would randomly show up at this moment.

"Moses is the one who received the Law on Mt. Sinai and led the children of Israel out of slavery, while Elijah is father of the Prophets," the angel explained. "Since by his imminent Passion, Death, and Resurrection, Jesus is about to free humankind from the ultimate slavery, which is sin, he is the fulfillment of both the Law and the Prophets, which point to him." Jenna was intrigued by depth of the connection between so many seemingly unrelated events.

Peter, James, and John, the only disciples present with Jesus on the mountain, were observing everything from a short distance away. At first their eyes appeared heavy as they sat on the ground with their shoulders slumped. But as the scene before them unfolded, they became animated and stood up, their eyes widening in awe. As Moses and Elijah were about to depart, Peter ran up to Jesus and said, "It's a good thing we are here. If you would like, we can make three tents for you, Moses, and Elijah."

While Peter was still speaking, a cloud came over them, casting a shadow all around them. The disciples froze, and their faces turned pale. As the cloud descended upon them, a loud voice thundered from within it, saying, "This is my Son, whom I love. Listen to him." When the cloud disappeared, Jesus and the disciples were alone. He touched each of their shoulders to reassure them because they still looked dazed.

Jenna sat down on the ground to take a few minutes to regain her strength, while her angel sat close by her side. Like Peter, she did not want to descend the mountain, but rather stay and linger in the place where Jesus had just been transfigured. For that brief moment, when Jesus' divinity shined through every fiber of his being, the brilliance of his light also burned through Jenna's doubts and fears. In the glory of that moment, anything seemed possible. Jesus appeared greater than any circumstance, even stronger than the power of death.

The pair gazed off toward the horizon in silence for some time. Then Jenna's angel leaned toward her, saying, "Even during this moment of great consolation, Jesus was pointing his disciples toward the Cross, strengthening them for what would come, and turning their gaze toward Jerusalem.

"Jenna, it is good to have mountaintop experiences in your spiritual life, like you are having right now. They can come in many forms — special time with family or friends, a moment of consolation in prayer, an encounter with Christ in the poor, a song that touches you deeply, a retreat where you experience God's presence, and countless other ways. These experiences can heighten your senses and deepen your relationship with Jesus. However, it is also important to know when to walk back down that mountain and pick up your cross, because it is on the road to Calvary that faith is tested and refined.

"Here on the Mountain of Transfiguration," he continued, "God provides reassurance that he understands the needs of his children. With Jesus' Passion and Death just around the corner, God knew that the leaders among the apostles needed to experience his glory in a tangible way.

"When your crosses seem too heavy, Jenna, when you feel that you are at your breaking point, remember that God's timing is impeccable. He will grant everything you need as you trust in his providence."

Sitting next to her angel, Jenna pondered all she had witnessed, and, for the first time, she felt truly grateful to be on this journey. It occurred to her that seeing firsthand these events in Jesus' life in the company of her guardian angel was, for her, in a sense, what the Transfiguration was for Peter, James, and John — a great consolation in the midst of difficult times. She imagined that the apostles would often return in their memories to each moment of their time with Jesus, just as she felt certain she would think back to this experience with her guardian angel in the challenging moments of her own life. After Jesus' death, she knew that the apostles would face many years of persecution and hard work, and it made sense that the Transfiguration would remind them that they were working for a kingdom that was not of this world.

Jenna had spent the past couple of years angry at God and trying to run from her crosses, but she was beginning to see that suffering came to everyone, even those closest to God. It was a beautiful thing to see God's glory, but what really mattered was what happened when you went back down that mountain. What would matter for Jenna was whether her life would change once this experience was over. There would be no shortcut, no easy way. She would have to learn, like the apostles, to trust God. And she already knew that this was lot easier said than done.

Sensing it was almost time to move on, Jenna slowly stood up. As if he understood the anxiety she was beginning to feel, knowing the Sorrowful Mysteries were nearly upon them, her angel gave her some words of encouragement. "For so many, Jenna, the Cross is a stumbling block, causing them to walk away from God's most precious gifts, because they are sometimes veiled behind mysteries difficult to accept. God doesn't promise to always spare us tough times, but he does promise to bring us through them and to bring good out of them in the end."

As they prayed the Glory Be, drawing the decade to a close, Jenna felt a new strength rising within her. She took her angel's hand, and, gazing out from the Mountain of Transfiguration, she offered her prayer. *"Lord, I pray for the confidence to know that you are with me at every moment, especially when life's storms begin to brew and my crosses seem too heavy. Help me to remember that there is no need for me to be anxious about the future, because your grace will be given to me at the precise moment I need it."*

Then the angel announced the final Mystery of Light, the bridge from Jesus' public ministry into his Passion and Death. "The fifth Luminous Mystery is The Institution of the Eucharist."

CHAPTER TWELVE

The Institution
of the Eucharist

'I am the living bread that came down from heaven; whoever eats this bread will live forever; and the bread that I will give is my flesh for the life of the world.' The Jews quarreled among themselves, saying, 'How can his man give us [his] flesh to eat?' Jesus said to them, 'Amen, amen, I say to you, unless you eat the flesh of the Son of Man and drink his blood, you do not have life within you. Whoever eats my flesh and drinks my blood has eternal life, and I will raise him on the last day. For my flesh is true food, and my blood is true drink' (John 6.51-55).

As they prayed the Our Father, Jenna felt her angel's hand on her shoulder and closed her eyes. As soon as she opened them, a solemn feeling overtook her, and she could sense the holiness of the mystery. Evening was falling and the two were alone. The angel informed her they were in the Upper Room in Jerusalem where the Last Supper would soon take place. The table was already prepared for the feast. He explained how he had wished for them to arrive before Jesus and the disciples, so that he could set the scene for Jenna against a backdrop of silence to help her fully experience this mystery.

The angel sat down, motioning for Jenna to join him on the floor by the long table in the spaces that Jesus and his disciples would soon occupy. They sat upright, facing one another. He reminded Jenna that it was the feast of Passover, when the Jews commemorated their Exodus from Egypt. They had long been living in oppressive slavery, but God heard their cries and, through Moses, delivered them from their plight. This was the holy night on which God called them out of Egypt and toward the Promised Land, when Moses parted the Red Sea.

The angel recalled for Jenna some of the details of the story from the Book of Exodus, which she had known as a child. He reminded her of the nine plagues that the Lord sent upon Egypt when Pharaoh refused Moses' request to free the Jews, and then the final tenth plague that immediately preceded their great departure. Then he recalled for her how God commanded the Jews to sacrifice an unblemished lamb, which they were to consume, and to put the blood of the sacrificial lamb on the two door posts and lintel of the houses in which they would eat it. He would spare them by the blood of the lamb.

The angel closed his eyes as he quoted from the Scriptural account: "For on this same night I will go through Egypt, striking down every firstborn in the land, human being and beast alike, and executing judgment on all the gods of Egypt — I, the LORD! But for you the blood will mark the houses where you are. Seeing the blood, I will pass over you; thereby, when I strike the land of Egypt, no destructive blow will come upon you. This day will be a day of remembrance for you, which your future generations will celebrate with pilgrimage to the LORD; you will celebrate it as a statute forever" (Exodus 12:12-14).

He explained that God also commanded that each year the Jews keep the custom of eating only unleavened bread, since the bread they were preparing did not have time to rise before their departure. "This was the feast that Jesus and his disciples had come to Jerusalem to commemorate, and it was during this feast that Jesus would institute the Eucharist," the angel said. "It would be his last meal before his Passion and Death."

The angel also reminded Jenna that the chief priests and scribes were looking for a way to put Jesus to death, because they were fearful of his growing popularity. Earlier, Judas had gone to them to discuss plans to hand

Jesus over in exchange for money, and was now searching for a time when there would be no crowd.

A chill came over Jenna at the mention of Judas' impending fall. It caused her to think back to the days when Justin embarked on his own dark path. She remembered how it was a slippery slope for him, one bad decision at a time, one small act of disobedience followed by a lie to cover up, until deception became the norm. By the time Justin ran away, he seemed like an altogether different person from the boy with whom Jenna grew up. He had become completely self-absorbed, oblivious to how deeply he was hurting those who loved him. *Had Judas gradually turned on Jesus, as well?* she wondered. *Was it one bad decision at a time, perhaps a misguided desire for power mixed with misunderstanding and festering anger that led to Judas' ultimate betrayal?*

Jenna continued to sit in silence across from her guardian angel, allowing all he had said to sink in and provide context for what she was about to witness. She thought back to her encounter with Jesus as a twelve-year-old boy, when, amidst the comfort and security of family and friends, he had come to Jerusalem to celebrate this same feast and had stayed behind in the Temple. He would have celebrated about twenty Passovers since that day.

***

It was evening, and Jesus and the Twelve were sitting around the table. Jenna stood beside her angel a short distance away to watch the scene unfold. While they were eating, Jesus said, "One of you sharing this meal with me will soon betray me."

Their jaws dropped, and they said, one after the other, "Not me, Lord!"

When Judas said it, Jesus' eyes became moist. "Hurry! Do what you must do, but do it quickly."

Jenna's eyes were glued to Jesus during his exchange with Judas. She saw his pain at being betrayed by one of his closest friends, and her heart went out to him. She knew all too well the stinging pain of betrayal from someone who is supposed to always be there for you. Jesus must have longed for Judas as Jenna longed for Justin. All she wanted was for Justin to be the young man she knew he could be — loyal, generous, protective. The person he had become in the past couple of years was not the real him. She had no doubt that Jesus, too, must have wanted Judas to be the man he could have been, not his betrayer.

"Although Jesus was deeply hurt, there was nothing that he would not have forgiven," the angel said. "Judas' biggest mistake was not his betrayal, but that he never sought the Lord's forgiveness. Soon after, he came to regret his decision and, giving into despair, he hanged himself." Jenna gasped. She hadn't remembered that part of the story.

"Whenever you fall, Jenna, always pick yourself up and run back to Jesus. There is nothing he will not forgive."

Jenna returned her attention to the Passover meal. The scene began to look familiar as Jesus took bread, said the blessing, broke it, and gave it to his disciples.

"Take this bread and eat it. This is my body."

Next he took a cup, gave thanks, and passed it to them.

"Drink from this cup, all of you. This is my blood, the blood of the New Covenant, which I will shed for the forgiveness of sins. Do this in memory of me."

Jenna recognized these words from what the priest says at Mass. Although she hadn't gone to Mass since her Confirmation two years ago, she was surprised to see how familiar the ritual still felt.

Jenna glanced up, and her eyes met the gaze of her faithful friend, who was looking intently in her direction. Sensing her angel had something more to say, and hoping he would help her unpack more of the elusive meaning that she sensed permeated this mysterious event, she waited silently for his words.

"The celebration of the Eucharist does more than simply recall the events of the Last Supper," he said in a slow, deliberate tone. "It makes present the Passion, Death, and Resurrection of Christ, offering their fruit to all who receive. The Mass is Christ's saving work continually re-presented to the Father for humankind, making the grace of these mysteries readily and tangibly accessible to people in every age. Before Jesus died, he desired to leave his followers a way to be mystically, yet truly, present at Calvary and to receive its benefits, which he won at so high a cost, as often as they wish.

"Therefore, Jenna, when you receive Holy Communion, it is not merely a symbolic gesture, but you are truly receiving the Body and Blood of Christ, given for you, and containing every blessing, because it is Jesus himself. Just as at the first Passover in Egypt the sacrificial lamb was consumed, so, too, are the children of the New Covenant given life when they consume Jesus, the Paschal Lamb. Moses led the children of Israel out of the slavery of Egypt, but Christ frees you from the slavery of sin."

The angel continued, "Jenna, there is no prayer more perfect or beautiful than the holy Mass, and receiving Jesus in the Eucharist draws you into the very life of God. Even in Heaven, you will not be closer to God than you are when you receive Communion. Therefore, confess your sins, so that you can fully receive every grace it brings.

"As you attend Mass, and as you spend time in the presence of Jesus before the Tabernacle, where Agnes spent so many hours, you will see the powerful transformation he will bring about in your life. Every friendship requires time together if it is to grow strong, and this is especially true of your friendship with God," the angel said. "Jesus promised he would remain with his disciples always, and he keeps this promise magnificently in the holy Eucharist."

As she contemplated the mystery, Jenna could not stop her thoughts from jumping ahead to the suffering Jesus would soon undergo. As she stood in the Upper Room that first Holy Thursday, she was struck by how fitting it was that bread and wine are the food offered to the Father at the Eucharistic sacrifice. Like wheat that is broken to make flour for bread, and grapes that are pressed to make wine, Jesus, too, would be broken and crushed for those who receive him.

She recalled how, upon his birth, Jesus was placed into a manger, a feeding trough, and the symbolism did not escape her. She remembered kneeling by the manger, looking upon him so tiny and vulnerable, and yet here he became, in a sense, even smaller. When her angel told her that Bethlehem means "House of Bread" in Hebrew, she was even further amazed at the ways of God. The same God who during the past few years of her life had seemed so distant suddenly felt very near.

"Jenna, Jesus knew that you would need help to live as he taught and here he provides it," the angel said. "It is not easy to forgive, to put others first and to trust God. In the

Eucharist Jesus strengthens his followers with his very self, his lifeblood." Jenna had always wondered why Agnes made such an effort to attend Mass every day, even when her body ached, and now she was beginning to understand.

Jenna turned her focus back to the scene before her. To her surprise, when the meal was over, an argument broke out among the disciples over which of them was the greatest. Jenna was surprised to see that they were still so far from understanding the significance of the meal they just shared, yet, at the same time, she was consoled that even the first disciples didn't understand everything all at once.

Jesus patiently taught them to the very end. "Those who don't know the heart of God lord their authority over others," he said. "But as for you, let the greatest among you be as the youngest, and the leader as the servant. Always remember that I came among you as one who serves."

Jesus locked eyes with Peter and said, "I have prayed that your faith may not fail. But once you have turned back, you must set an example and strengthen your brothers."

"Lord, I would die for you," Peter said.

"Peter, before the cock crows this day, you will deny me three times." Peter grew pale and slowly shook his head, holding Jesus' gaze.

So much had happened in this mystery, and Jenna was struggling to process all she had witnessed. But since this mystery was intimately connected with those still to come, she hoped she would understand better as the rest of the mysteries unfolded. After a few moments, the angel bowed his head as a signal for Jenna to conclude the final Luminous Mystery.

After seeing Jesus give himself so completely, Jenna could think of nothing left to ask for. With hands folded, she took a moment to search her heart but every prayer that came to mind seemed inadequate. After a few moments, she gave voice to the prayer that formed within her. *"Lord, I am sorry for all of the times that I took your love and your gifts for granted, and for the times I called Mass boring because I never knew what was truly taking place. Although I cannot fully comprehend this mystery, help me to trust in your love, which knows no bounds."*

Then the angel solemnly announced "The first Sorrowful Mystery is The Agony in the Garden."

The Sorrowful Mysteries

CHAPTER THIRTEEN

The Agony in the Garden

Amen, amen, I say to you, you will weep and mourn, while the world rejoices; you will grieve, but your grief will become joy. When a woman is in labor, she is in anguish because her hour has arrived; but when she has given birth to a child, she no longer remembers the pain because of her joy that a child has been born into the world. So you also are now in anguish. But I will see you again, and your hearts will rejoice, and no one will take your joy away from you. On that day you will not question me about anything. Amen, amen, I say to you, whatever you ask the Father in my name he will give you (John 16:20-23).

As they began the first Sorrowful Mystery, Jenna's heart was heavy. She watched Jesus make his way from the Upper Room, where he had just shared his Last Supper with the disciples, into the Garden of Gethsemane, and her throat grew tight. She knew they were entering the mysteries where Jesus would suffer his Passion and Death, and she was afraid she would not have the strength to watch the horrific events unfold.

As her knees grew weak, her guardian angel came up beside her and took her by the hand. As he firmly wrapped his hand around her own, his strength seemed to hold her up.

Jenna watched the disciples follow Jesus into the Garden. They seemed to be in a daze, perhaps still shaken from his words to them in the Upper Room. God's plan was becoming increasingly difficult to comprehend.

"My soul is sorrowful to the point of death," Jesus said. "Stay here and watch with me."

Then he went off a little ways, taking with him Peter, James, and John, the same disciples whom he had taken to Mount Tabor for the Transfiguration. The angel led Jenna by the hand, and the two followed Jesus, watching him while he prayed. A look of profound sorrow spread across his face, and his shoulders drooped, as if a heavy weight had been cast upon them. He summoned the strength to turn his tormented gaze toward Heaven, and then he dropped to his knees and prayed, "Father, take this cup of suffering away from me." Then he added, "Yet not what I want, but your will be done." His agony was so great and his prayer so fervent that drops of sweat mixed with blood fell from his forehead.

When he prayed, an angel appeared to Jesus and held him tenderly. At the angel's appearance, a look of resignation and deep love came upon his face. He got up and went back to his disciples, who were sound asleep.

"Peter, could you not stay awake with me for even one hour? Watch and pray that you may not be put to the test. The spirit is willing, but the flesh is weak."

Jenna looked at the angel, her eyes filled with tears, then back at Jesus in his agony. The angel removed his hand from Jenna's and wrapped his arm gently around her shoulders. He was standing so close that he was almost embracing her. Although that was the first time the angel stood that close, the comfort he brought felt familiar, as if he had often been invisibly at her side, embracing her in the difficult moments of her life. In that instant Jenna understood just how near he had always been.

Somewhat surprised at this knowledge, which came more like a forgotten memory than new information, she glanced up at her angel, who seemed to be reading her thoughts. He smiled back in a way that confirmed her intuition. He looked pleased that Jenna was becoming aware of realities unknown to so many.

Feeling again the closeness and provision of God, Jenna's strength was renewed, and she turned her full focus back to Jesus. *Why did he suffer so intensely during his prayer? Was it the anticipation of what was coming that caused him to sweat blood, or was it something more?*

"Why will the Father not answer his Son's prayer and take away that suffering?" she asked her angel. "There must be another way," she said, almost pleading.

As Jenna struggled to comprehend so great a mystery as man's redemption through the Cross, the angel tried to help her understand. "In this moment, Jesus is carrying in his soul the weight of all sin. The suffering of his Passion goes far beyond the physical torment he endured, as horrific as that was, to one that can only be seen with eyes of faith. Jesus is taking upon himself every transgression ever committed, knowing that death, sin's inevitable consequence, is not far off. Yet this is why he came: to carry mankind's sin to the Cross for it to be nailed there, and to undergo death in order to conquer it.

"There is no shortcut, Jenna," the angel continued. "You are witnessing the most significant battle ever fought. Sin, death, and all their power are unleashed against Jesus, who responds only with love and acceptance of the Father's will. He is erasing the prideful disobedience of Adam in the first Garden with his humble obedience in this one, revealing the depths of his love."

Jenna listened closely, feeling so small before so great a mystery, yet also so important and loved.

"He does this for all humankind, but also for each and every person. Jesus is taking on your sin, too, Jenna, as well as all the sin ever committed against you."

Jenna shared with the angel a memory she suddenly recalled of something her mother said the night Agnes died. "I wish I could take that pain from you and carry it myself."

The angel nodded, the sorrow from the memory of that night fresh in his eyes. "Because he is both God and man, Jesus can and does take on your pain. He carries the pain of death and separation, loneliness, fear, physical distress, and every other suffering that you can know. Jesus intimately understands your concern for Justin, the anguish you feel over your family's brokenness, and your sorrow at losing Agnes.

"He doesn't merely endure suffering, but his imminent victory will provide the antidote. He will conquer death with love, pride with humility, darkness with truth, and infidelity with perseverance to the bitter end." *Could this really be God's response to sin and suffering?*

Even as the angel spoke, Jenna's eyes remained fixed on Jesus. While he was speaking to his disciples, Judas arrived with a crowd carrying torches and swords. He went over to Jesus and kissed him.

"Judas, must you betray me with a kiss?"

When his disciples realized what was happening, one of them drew a sword and struck one of the soldiers that approached Jesus, cutting off his ear.

"Stop!" Jesus said. Then he touched the man's ear and healed him.

Jesus addressed the soldiers. "Why have you come after me with weapons, as though I am a criminal? I have been with you, day after day, teaching in the Temple area and you never arrested me. But this is the hour of the power of darkness." Then they arrested Jesus and took him away.

Jenna and her angel stood in the darkness and silence that covered the Garden of Gethsemane. Everyone had scattered, and she could see Peter following Jesus from a safe distance. Jenna's mouth went dry. Earlier, Jesus had known where Judas was going. He could have easily evaded the soldiers. Wasn't there another way to redeem humankind?

After a few moments, the angel's voice pierced the profound silence as he led her in the Glory Be. Then he said, "Before we follow Jesus into the next mystery, what would you like to pray for?"

After a brief period of reflection, Jenna prayed, *"Father, may I learn to love your will above my own, even when I don't understand, and trust always that you know what is best. I don't understand why certain things had to happen in my life, but help me to see how you are with me and working through it all."*

And with her prayer, the angel announced, "The second Sorrowful Mystery is The Scourging at the Pillar."

CHAPTER FOURTEEN

The Scourging at the Pillar

He was spurned and avoided by men,
a man of suffering, knowing pain,
Like one from whom you turn your face,
spurned, and we held him in no esteem.

Yet it was our pain that he bore,
our sufferings he endured.
We thought of him as stricken,
struck down by God and afflicted...
(Isaiah 53:3-4).

After announcing the mystery, the angel promptly began the prayers, keeping Jenna on task. After the Our Father, Jenna's courage increased, and she went with the angel, whose arm was still draped around her shoulders, to follow Jesus to his first trial.

They stood about ten feet away from Jesus as the soldiers led him away. "They are taking him to the house of Caiaphas, the high priest, where the chief priests, elders, and scribes are gathered for a secret trial by night," the angel explained.

When they arrived, there were men who testified against him, one by one, but their stories conflicted, so they could not convict him. Jesus remained silent the whole time.

Finally, Caiaphas asked him directly, "Are you the Messiah? Are you the Son of God?"

Jenna's eyes were fixed on Jesus, whom she knew could never deny who he was. "I am."

At Jesus' response, Caiaphas tore his garments and condemned him for blasphemy. "We have heard him for ourselves. We have no further need of testimony," he said. Then some of them blindfolded Jesus, beat him, and mocked him, saying, "So you think you're a prophet? Then who is it that struck you?!"

After the ordeal was over, the angel took Jenna, shaken by the violence she had witnessed, to the courtyard where Peter, following along at a distance, was warming himself by a fire. A young woman came in and recognized him as one of Jesus' followers, but Peter denied knowing him. Soon after, two others recognized

Peter as a friend of Jesus, but two more times Peter denied him.

After he denied him for the third time, the cock crowed, and Jesus looked at Peter. Peter then went off and wept bitterly, and Jenna remembered Jesus' prediction at the Last Supper that Peter would deny him three times before the cock crowed.

***

The next morning, Caiaphas tied together Jesus' hands. Jenna winced as she saw the bruises and dried blood that covered his body from the beatings of the previous night. The angel explained how Caiaphas was sending him to Pilate to be tried for claiming to be a king. Caiaphas did not have the authority to execute, so Jesus was being sent to Pilate for another trial, which Caiaphas hoped would end in a death sentence. Israel was under the rule of Rome, and Caiaphas knew that Pilate would put to death anyone who appeared to threaten Caesar's authority.

When Jesus arrived, Pilate, along with a large crowd that had gathered, was waiting for him. Pilate asked Jesus if he was indeed King of the Jews.

"You say that I am."

As the chief priests proceeded to accuse Jesus of all sorts of things, Pilates' eyes darted back and forth between the priests and Jesus, who remained silent.

"Although he was surprised by Jesus' silence," the angel explained, "Pilate saw through Caiaphas and the chief priests and knew they had only sent Jesus to him because their own law didn't permit them to put a man to death."

When the crowd asked Pilate for the release of a prisoner, as the angel explained was the custom at Passover, Pilate suggested that he release Jesus. But the chief priests incited them to ask for Barabbas, whom the angel told Jenna was a rebel who had committed murder.

"Then what do you want me to do with Jesus?" Pilate asked, shifting nervously.

The crowd shot him a thunderous response. "Crucify him!"

Eventually, Pilate caved under the pressure and gave in to their demands. He released Barabbas and handed Jesus over to the Roman soldiers to be scourged and crucified.

Jenna wondered how her knees did not buckle beneath her. The soldiers, like hungry dogs, finally let loose on their prey, grabbed him, and threw him against a pillar while the crowd shouted on in vicious approval. They fastened Jesus' already bound hands to the top of the pillar and began the merciless scourging with their instruments of torture.

Jenna could not endure any more. She looked up at her angel with tears flowing down her face. The angel looked tenderly back at Jenna, and, moving even closer, wrapped his long wings around her entire body, so that only her face was showing. The angel's wings seemed to contain love and strength, so that, surrounded by their power and within their safety, Jenna could get through the scenes that lay ahead. She knew she would not have been able to bear it otherwise.

Secure in her angel's embrace, Jenna was able to reflect on the scene before her. She wondered why the means for redemption had to be so messy. *Couldn't Jesus have conquered sin without so much blood and violence?* She struggled anew to reconcile her image of a loving Father with the scene before her. In Gethsemane, Jesus prayed for the Father's will to be done. *How could such a prayer lead to this?* She confided her questions to the angel.

"Redemption was messy, Jenna, because sin is messy," he said with a sadness in his voice she had never heard.

"You are witnessing the horror of sin, the manifestation of its true colors. If ever you doubt the effects of sin — of pride, infidelity, selfishness, lust, greed, to name a few of its roots — you have only to look upon Jesus during his Passion," he said. "So many take sin casually, thinking of it is as a personal or hidden matter. But it blocks the blessings that God so desires to bestow upon you and shatters your relationship with God and with those you hurt. It is a lack of love for your neighbor, yourself, and ultimately God, who made you for the greatness of true and pure love.

"Jesus' beautiful response to this reality is to take sin upon himself, with the pain and death it brings, in order to conquer it through divine love. Only Jesus Christ, true God and true man, could have done this. Only the Word of God, through whom creation came into being, could have restored it."

The angel paused for a few moments, his eyes fixed on Jesus. "You are witnessing sin being unleashed against Our Lord's body. You can see its effects in the world, too. Its fruit is division, pain, and death. Too often people reject God's will, taking what appears to be the easy or more pleasurable path, which later brings so much grief. But Jesus shows you the path of self-sacrifice and humility, modeling a depth of love that the world had never seen. This is the power that restored humanity, and, like a candle in the darkness, lights the way back to life with God.

"However, without losing sight of the ugliness of sin, Jenna, you should never lose heart at your shortcomings. God always responds to the weakness of his children with grace. Look at the lengths he goes to in order to be with you," the angel said motioning toward Jesus, no longer recognizable from the beatings.

As the angel spoke, his face was right next to Jenna's. His words penetrated her heart, because God's love was no longer an abstract concept, but she could see it before her eyes. Jenna had experienced enough pain to realize that she needed a savior who could meet her in her hardships and provide more than mere words. She knew the havoc sin had wreaked in a world torn apart by war, terrorism, greed, and hunger, causing even the most innocent to suffer. Humankind could not make its way back to God and know true peace without concrete help.

Jenna took her eyes off of Jesus for a moment and allowed her gaze to settle upon the crowd. She noticed Mary amidst the mass of observers, closely following everything, and Jenna's heart broke. She thought of Mary tenderly holding the Baby Jesus in the stable in Bethlehem and lovingly protecting him from the dust as she brought him into the Temple to be consecrated to his Father. Now, Mary could only watch as he suffered in the flesh she herself had given him.

When Jenna looked upon Mary, her body became tense, and the angel followed her gaze over to where the Blessed Mother stood. He could offer no words of consolation. He simply bowed his head in silent reverence.

The sorrow of this scene stood in sharp contrast to the joy that accompanied the Annunciation. Here, there was no angel announcing God's plan, no miracle being proclaimed. This mystery required faith in its purest form. Jenna was beginning to understand that to love

Jesus was to love him, not only in the good times, but from amidst her suffering and darkness, as he loved her from amidst his. His eyes seemed to ask for her trust, even when she didn't understand how anything good could possibly come from her own trials.

After some time, Jenna and her angel prayed the Glory Be, bringing the decade to a close. Then the angel waited as Jenna formulated the prayer that was in her heart. *"Lord, help me to better recognize my own sin, so that I may confess it and receive the grace to overcome my weaknesses. And help me to trust that you are at work, even in the darkest moments of my life when nothing makes sense."*

Then the angel announced, "The third Sorrowful Mystery is The Crowning with Thorns."

CHAPTER FIFTEEN

The Crowning with Thorns

But he was pierced for our sins,
crushed for our iniquity.
He bore the punishment that makes us whole,
by his wounds we were healed
(Isaiah 53:5).

Jenna and her angel walked slowly alongside Jesus as Pilate's soldiers led him into the palace after his scourging, where they further ridiculed him. The soldiers ripped off his clothes, reopening his wounds from the scourging, and threw a dirty, scarlet cloak around him. Then they weaved a crown from sharp thorns, placed it on his head, and gave him a reed to hold. Kneeling before him in mockery, they cried, "Hail, King of the Jews." Then, taking the reed from his hand, they struck his head with it and spat on him.

Jenna stood back and looked at Jesus, so badly beaten and covered in blood that he was barely recognizable. Yet even through the disfigurement from the beatings and lashes, and all the blood that dripped down his face from the crown of thorns, Jenna could still find his eyes, burning with love, asking for her love in return.

Jesus did not keep himself at a safe distance, demanding her trust from afar. He entered her suffering. He was not a high and mighty king wearing a crown of gold and a royal cloak, barking orders and using his power for selfish purposes. Jesus wore a crown of sharp thorns and a filthy cloak, calling to her with his hands bound, offering his life for her.

Far from wanting to turn away, she could not take her eyes off him. She felt her heart drawn to him as if by some magnetic force. There, in that moment, through his complete self-offering, Jesus was speaking a language that Jenna's heart understood. She knew deep inside that, no matter what the cost, he would always be her King. Jenna's moment of decision had come. The doubts with which she began this journey were washed away in the tidal wave of his love.

The angel, too, was gazing upon Jesus in this unspeakable state. He allowed some time to pass before he spoke. "In this mystery, Jesus is suffering the fruit of man's pride and arrogance," he said. "Without realizing it, the soldiers not only mocked Jesus, but also his identity as Messiah. The irony is that they could not impede his mission, because it was through his suffering that he would save humanity.

"Many in Israel were expecting the Messiah to be a conquering king who would free them from the violent oppression of Rome. In the past, their great kings, such as David, had always conquered their enemies. But although they could not yet see it, God had given them so much more. Jesus was indeed a conquering king, but his triumph came through suffering and rejection, and his victory was not over any specific regime, but over sin and death.

"In Heaven, where there is no pain, Jesus reigns in a kingdom where there is only love in its purest form," the angel continued. "Prepare yourself to live in this kingdom, Jenna, while you are still on Earth. Your ultimate end is to one day be with him in paradise, where pure and selfless love reigns. But this kind of love must be learned in this life."

Jenna thought about her own pride and how, at times, she put her own comfort or popularity above what she knew was right. She recalled times, both at school and at home, when she was so absorbed in her own problems that she ignored the pain around her. She sometimes took part in conversations that put others down in order to feel superior, or participated in vain competition that tore others down, rather than healthy competition that inspired and built them up. She also remembered times she lashed out at loved ones because things weren't going her way. And too often she expected God to fix her problems in her way and on her timeline, as if he were her servant rather than her Lord, when she should have been trusting in his ways and timing.

As she resolved in her heart to do better, she found herself dropping to her knees to pay homage to the King as he endured the rest of the soldiers' jeering. A deep peace rested upon her like a heavy blanket, and it took her by surprise that she could feel so much peace in the midst of such suffering. When the soldiers were finished, they put Jesus back in his own clothes and led him off to his execution.

As the mystery came to a close, Jenna, still on her knees, bowed her head and began her prayer. *"Lord, may I always remember that in your kingdom you reign with love and humility that know no bounds. Teach me to love like you.'*

The angel tenderly placed his hand on Jenna's shoulder. "The fourth Sorrowful Mystery is The Carrying of the Cross."

CHAPTER SIXTEEN

The Carrying of the Cross

We had all gone astray like sheep,
all following our own way;
But the LORD laid upon him
the guilt of us all.

Seized and condemned, he was taken away.
Who would have thought any more of his destiny?
For he was cut off from the land of the living,
struck for the sins of his people
(Isaiah 53:6, 8).

As the soldiers brought the Cross to Jesus, Jenna rose from her knees. He was so weakened from the beatings that he could barely stay on his feet. Yet despite

147

his fatigue, Jesus straightened his back and tenderly caressed the Cross, as if receiving a long-awaited friend.

As Jesus embraced the Cross, Jenna looked into his eyes. A light shone through them that could not be extinguished. The soldiers placed the heavy Cross on his back and, although his steps were slow, his gaze was fixed on Calvary. He was determined to accomplish the task at hand, pushed along by love alone.

As Jesus struggled to put one foot in front of the other, Jenna felt her heart break, knowing he was carrying her sins, as well. Looking upon Jesus, she resolved once again to do better and to make amends for her failings.

Lasting happiness, Jenna was discovering, does not come from taking the easy path, but the right path and trusting that God will be there. She thought about how Agnes chose to trust God every day, especially during those years as a single mom, and she was beginning to understand where she found the strength.

After going a short distance, the Roman soldiers feared that Jesus might not make it to Calvary. They grabbed a passerby, whom the angel told her was Simon of Cyrene, a farmer coming in from the fields, and forced him to carry the Cross for Jesus. Simon hesitantly received the Cross, drenched in the Lord's sweat and blood, and took it upon himself.

As Jesus made his way toward Mount Calvary, Jenna and the angel journeyed alongside him. Her heart was heavy, but when the angel spoke, the sound of his voice brought her comfort. "When you have crosses to carry, Jenna, whether large or small, when suffering comes your way, or even small annoyances, learn from Jesus how to carry them well, so that they may be fruitful," he said.

"While you should always do what you can to eliminate injustice and suffering, pain inevitably finds its way into everyone's life. If, in your heart, you unite your suffering to the Cross of Christ, its power will be immeasurable, because Jesus sanctified suffering."

The angel's words called to mind a memory of Agnes. Sometimes when Jenna would visit, she could see that Agnes was suffering from the physical effects of a long life filled with hard work. Jenna would feel badly, but Agnes never felt sorry for herself. She shared with Jenna her belief that suffering was precious in God's eyes, because it could be offered to him as a sign of love and trust.

Jenna didn't quite understand what she meant, but just the same, once in a while, when she could see that Agnes was hurting, she would ask, "Who are you offering it for this time?" One time, Agnes' response stopped her in tracks. "Today, it's all for you, my friend."

As Jenna watched Jesus, she confided to the angel that she wished she could be Simon, helping him in his darkest hour. "Jenna, if you truly wish to help Jesus in his time of need, just look around you. Jesus' love for his children runs so deeply that when you help another, it is as though you were helping him," he said. "And when people are there for you, they, too, are like Simon of Cyrene.

"This is true whether you assist someone in a simple way, like when you would help Agnes with chores, or in a way that requires more courage," the angel continued. "If you ask God to show you those who are most in need of help, you might be surprised by what he will reveal."

When the angel said this, the faces of many kids who carry heavy burdens flashed through Jenna's mind, but there was one girl in particular whom she could not stop thinking about. Jenna met Maggie the day she transferred into her new school. Maggie often seemed to be on the peripheral, not having many friends. Although she was a bit eccentric and distant, Maggie was the first person to talk to Jenna at her new school, and Jenna had always been grateful for her kindness.

A few months later, for no reason that Jenna could see, some kids began making Maggie the butt of their jokes, and their teasing quickly escalated. Their taunting seemed to take on a life of its own as others joined in a weak attempt to boost their own popularity or to protect themselves from becoming the next target. Their harassment didn't stop at school but continued over the internet, making it impossible for Maggie to escape.

The angel invited Jenna to look more closely at Jesus as he struggled beneath the weight of the Cross. Each step he took looked as though it could be his last. As Jenna looked upon Jesus, burdened and rejected, she suddenly saw in his face the image of Maggie's, and it appeared as though Jesus and Maggie were one in their suffering.

The memory of the crowd that cried out for Jesus' death, with his mother standing in its midst unable to stop the tide, flashed into Jenna's mind. As she recalled the angry mob, for a brief moment she could see Maggie, alone in her room, sitting before her computer and reading in tears the insults hurled against her. The more Maggie read, the heavier Jesus' steps became, until finally he came crashing to the ground, the Cross landing hard upon his back and his head, which was still crowned with thorns.

As she caught a glimpse of the true effects of such cruelty, Jenna stood motionless. She thought about what it meant for Jesus to carry our sins. In some mysterious way, he truly carried the sins committed against Maggie, and in so doing, he also carried Maggie's pain. In that moment, she saw that somehow Jesus truly does go before us into our darkest times.

Although Jenna hadn't participated in the teasing, and even at times tried to encourage Maggie through a smile or kind word, there on the road to Calvary with Jesus, she knew she should have done more. She may not have been able to stop their behavior, but she was certain that if her love for Jesus and for Maggie had been stronger, she would have done more. She promised herself that when she returned to school after Christmas vacation, she would be different.

"Jenna, there are no shortage of opportunities to help Jesus in his time of need," the angel said. "His closest followers abandoned him out of fear and were not there as he carried the Cross to Calvary. But in your life, you can be there for him by being there for others, as Agnes was there for you with her faith and wisdom, helping you to carry your cross.

"Pray for those who carry heavy burdens and ask God how he may be calling you to alleviate some of the suffering in the world. There are many people who would trade every possession for the gift of living free of chronic pain or sickness for just one day," he said. "Even today, so many people go to bed hungry and face life without the simplest medical care. For others, loneliness and isolation weigh heavily upon them every day.

"In some areas of the world, to follow Christ is to risk torture and death," he said. "In your culture, there are crosses that come with simply trying to live as Jesus taught — to respect every person and to stand for life. But God always offers abundant grace to those who seek his ways.

"Your own struggles are infinitely important to God, but he also wants to pull you beyond your own pain. There is healing in helping others," he said.

The angel's words lifted Jenna's spirits. They brought hope that she had the power to do something truly important with her life. Although she didn't yet know what that would be, she began to feel optimistic about her future. She wanted her time on this Earth to matter.

As Jenna and her angel prayed the Glory Be, bringing to a close the fourth decade of the Sorrowful Mysteries, Jenna looked ahead and saw that they were about to ascend Mount Calvary. Realizing they would soon arrive at the next mystery, she stopped to offer her prayer.

"Lord, may I always carry my crosses in life with patience and love, and when I serve others, help me to remember that it is you I am serving."

Then they silently ascended the final distance to the summit of Mount Calvary. When they arrived at the top of the hill, the two stopped and dropped to their knees. Jenna tried to brace herself for what was coming next. After a long silence, the angel solemnly announced, "The fifth Sorrowful Mystery is The Crucifixion."

CHAPTER SEVENTEEN

The Crucifixion

This is my commandment: love one another as I love you. No one has greater love than this, to lay down one's life for one's friends (John 15:12-13).

As the scene continued before them, Jenna and her guardian angel stood up and began the prayers of the last and most solemn of the Sorrowful Mysteries.

Once Jesus made it to the top of the hill, he collapsed to the ground from exhaustion and from his weakened state. Even with Simon's help, Jesus could barely make the arduous journey. Yet beneath the suffering, a look of deep purpose remained upon his face, as if he were that much closer to accomplishing the task for which he was born.

The soldiers did not give him even a brief moment to regain his strength. They immediately shoved him onto the wood, slamming his bleeding body against the Cross.

He could barely lie back onto it, so raw were the wounds on his back from the scourging.

Jenna could not watch anymore. She hid her face from the soldiers' brutality and threw herself back into the safety of her guardian angel's embrace. He once again wrapped her in his majestic wings, and with renewed strength she let her gaze return to the Crucifixion.

The soldiers moved swiftly and efficiently, allowing little time for the resistance one might expect when carrying out such a task. However, even the hardened soldiers were distracted momentarily as they watched, with jaws dropped, while Jesus tenderly opened his arms onto the crossbeam, as if embracing all humanity.

As they drove the nails into his hands and feet and raised up on the Cross the Creator of the universe, rather than words of condemnation, he prayed, "Father, forgive them. They do not know what they are doing."

Jenna had heard those famous words of mercy before, but standing in the power of that moment and seeing forgiveness radiate from his eyes amidst such torment and rejection, for the first time she truly *heard* them. She understood that his forgiveness extended not only to the soldiers crucifying him, but to all people, for it was not only the soldiers' sins, but everyone's, that nailed him to that tree.

From the Cross, Jesus laid bare the heights and depths of God's love, a love so much greater than the world had ever known, yet in its supreme moment it remained unrecognizable to most. Jesus' words showed Jenna a glimpse of the heart of God, who, in loving the world so completely, was utterly rejected. Yet still he chose to forgive, for it was man's rejection of God that Jesus was taking upon himself. God's ways were indeed mysterious, yet never so visible.

In addition to receiving forgiveness, Jenna felt rising in her heart the desire and power to release those whose mistakes had hurt her. It felt like a lead jacket was removed from her shoulders as she let go of the betrayal and abandonment she carried from Justin's addiction and running away, resentment at the loss of her old school and neighborhood, the turmoil that came with her parents' divorce, and her anger at God for taking Agnes and letting so many bad things happen in her life.

Jenna's eyes remained glued to the Cross. She watched the soldiers divide his garments by casting lots, then fasten above his head a sign that read, "This is Jesus, the King of the Jews." Then they sat down to keep guard.

There was a group watching from a short distance away who ridiculed him. "If he is really the Messiah, let's see him save himself!" The soldiers also mocked him.

Jenna looked into Jesus' eyes and saw pain renewed at each jeer. Heartbroken, she looked up at her angel, who placed his hand on her shoulder. "Jesus' heart could never be hardened," he said. "Far from being immune to the taunting and rejection, it broke a little more with each jab." Jenna wondered how she could ever have thought God was absent from her life and indifferent to suffering.

There were two criminals who had been crucified with Jesus, one on each side of him. One of the criminals joined the others in their taunting. "If you are the Messiah, save yourself and us."

But the other said to him, "Have you no fear of God? We were punished justly for our crimes, but this man has done nothing wrong." Then he said, "Jesus, remember me when you come into your kingdom."

The criminal's act of trust seemed to console Jesus. "I assure you, today you will be with me in Paradise," he said.

Jenna looked up at the criminal, who had been so hostile on his journey to Calvary. Now his whole demeanor had changed. He would die in peace. The world had given up on him, but Jesus believed in him until the end.

Then she looked over at the criminal who had rejected Jesus, his face so contorted from bitterness and anger that he no longer appeared human. Jenna was puzzled and asked, "Why won't he turn to Jesus like the other criminal? How can he not see that there is forgiveness for him, too?"

The angel also appeared bewildered. He stepped back to where he could take in the entire scene, gently releasing Jenna from his wings.

After a few moments, he answered, "Now we are entering the mystery of man's free will. God will never impose himself upon anyone, but each person must decide whether to turn away from sin, or from God and his ways of humility and selflessness. God created you with free will, and he will never interfere with that sacred gift.

"So many people make light of sin," the angel continued. "Jenna, never make light of sin. Look at the Cross and see its consequences. When you become aware of your transgressions, confess them and run back into your Father's arms. God's mercy is limitless, and he is always ready to forgive and restore. But when you turn your heart from God, you are in danger of becoming like this criminal, who is so hardened that, although Jesus is right there offering his mercy, he will not accept it.

"Little by little, one decision at a time, you become more attached to your sin. God's mercy then appears foreign and even undesirable, and you begin to justify your actions, no longer recognizing right from wrong," the angel said, visibly saddened by this reality. "When you conduct yourself in a way that is far from God's will, you turn away from his light, preferring darkness and secrecy where your actions won't be seen."

Jenna stood almost in fright of the power of man's free will. "Why does God allow this to happen? Is our freedom so important that he would let us choose such misery, cause such pain, and ultimately require the Crucifixion of his Son for our redemption?"

The angel looked so intently at Jenna that she felt as though he was looking right through her. "Jenna, think about what would happen if you were not free, how different you would be." He paused for a moment. "Without freedom, you would be like a robot programmed to act a certain way, and your life would not truly be your own. You would not know the joy that comes with loving and being loved, because true love must always be rooted in freedom. Your love is so important to God that it is worth all this to him," he said, gesturing toward the Cross. "But each person must decide for himself how generously he will respond to God's invitation."

Jenna thought about Justin and the amazing brother he had been for so many years. Her heart ached for him, knowing he was making one bad decision after another. She prayed that he would not become like the hardened criminal.

With undying optimism in his voice, as if sensing her concern, the angel added, "Keep praying for even the most hardened of people, Jenna. There is always hope. Never give up on anyone, even if it appears that all is lost. God's grace can break through even at the very last moment, as it did with the good thief."

At the angel's words, Jenna felt a surge of hope for Justin's recovery. But even if her biggest fear was realized, she found comfort in knowing that Jesus would be by his side until the very end. If Jesus had gone through all this for Justin, he would never abandon him in his time of need.

Jenna returned her attention to the Cross. She could see that, with each breath, new waves of pain shot through Jesus' body. Yet as Jenna watched this horrific suffering, she could also see in his eyes the love that gave it power.

"It would be so easy to turn away from the agony in this scene and conclude that God could never be present in such a place," the angel said. "Yet to do this would be to miss a great paradox of Christianity: Although it is impossible for God to sin, he found a way to meet you in your darkest moments and heal you at the root, showing that his love and mercy know no bounds.

"All the power of sin and death came against Jesus in full force as he hung upon the Cross that Friday afternoon," the angel continued, his words inevitably falling short of the beautiful reality he was attempting to describe. "God's mysterious plan was being realized. Healing and redemption were at long last coming to a lost and broken world from a tree, just as sin and death entered the world through the fruit of another ancient tree. The far-reaching consequences of one man's pride and disobedience were reversed by the humility and obedience of another, God's own Son. And he made available to all the fruit of his sacrifice the night before his death, when he gave his followers in every age the means to receive his Body and Blood.

"At the stable in Bethlehem, his cradle had appropriately been a feeding trough, and now his throne was a Cross. Jesus, the Paschal Lamb, became both high priest and victim, offering himself as the final sacrifice."

The angel's simple, yet revealing, words gave rise to new courage in Jenna. She boldly approached the Cross and dropped to her knees, resting her forehead against its base. She felt as though she could not get close enough, wanting the love and the power that were flowing forth from Christ to flow through to the very depths of her being.

She thought back to the first time she knelt before him. At the manger, she beheld Jesus small and vulnerable, teaching her volumes without a word. This time, her encounter was very different as she knelt before him, even further emptied of his glory.

As she looked up at Jesus, she saw his choice to love renewed with each painful movement. Being God, he could have come down from that Cross at any moment, but love alone kept him there. All the love songs ever written didn't even come close to describing this reality.

Seeing Jesus offer himself at such great personal cost made Jenna realize the false nature of things which at times she mistook for love or intimacy. With Christ's sacrifice shining before her like a beacon, she began to think about some of the things she had done to gain the affection of others, who did not even have her best interest at heart, when it was really the love of God for which she was longing.

She thought of the false masks she sometimes wore to appear as though she had everything together, hiding her true self to gain approval from others. She also recalled with regret a time when, because her parents were preoccupied with Justin, she was able to stay out much later than normal. She spent the evening with a boy she really liked and let things go too far, giving a little too much of herself, because he offered her the attention and affection she craved.

A profound sadness came over Jenna as she also thought about other kids she knew whose lives would be so different if they knew they were loved to this degree. As her angel stepped back, bowing his head in prayer during this beautiful moment in her young life, her thoughts turned into a heartfelt prayer for so many whom she loved. Memories of people she had long forgotten made their way back into her consciousness, and she entrusted each one to the Lord in his hour of supreme mercy.

When Jenna rose from her knees, the angel came close, as if he knew there was something she needed to say. She told him about some kids from school and some of their struggles. She knew so many who were seeking love in such dangerous ways.

Some had turned to drugs and alcohol to mask the pain in their lives, some to promiscuity, mistaking physical intimacy for love. For others, it was more subtle. They were obsessed with being the best in the classroom or on the playing field in order to feel that they were valuable, not knowing their infinite value in God's eyes. Still others would continually spend all their money on clothes or expensive possessions in an effort to fill the emptiness in their heart, which God alone can fill, when so much good could be done if they would give more to the poor.

With great sadness, Jenna recalled a girl from her old school with whom she would talk from time to time. She always wore a long sweater to cover the wounds on her arms that she had sustained from cutting herself. She once told Jenna the reason she did it was that it made her feel alive.

Tears filled Jenna's eyes as she looked up at the Cross and then back at the angel. "If they knew how much they were loved, things would be so different."

As Jenna spoke, the angel listened wholeheartedly, following her every word. In her angel's eyes, Jenna could see Heaven's compassion for these children. The angel took Jenna into his arms, and the two wept together.

"Can't you take them here, too, so that they can learn what I now know?" she asked her angel.

"Jenna, you have the power to take them here yourself, in the same way that Agnes took you. You can bring them to the Cross through your prayers, and by the way you live they will come to see that there is another way. Over time they will come to know God's love through you, as you tasted it through Agnes," he said. "God himself will work in and through you in ways that you cannot even imagine, because he longs for their happiness even more than you do.

"The effects of sin in the world are real — division, betrayal, oppression, war, terrorism, random shootings, and so much other pain that wreaks havoc in the world and in people's lives. But here at the Cross, God shows that he is with you in your suffering and that hatred and death will not have the last word.

"People suffer to different degrees, but nobody is exempt from sin's ultimate fruit: death. Through the Cross, Christ brings a broken world back into the arms of its loving Father. His most eloquent homily is delivered, not from a pulpit, but from the Cross. This love requires a response from every person, who must decide if he will persist in selfishness, heaping more pain upon the world, or embrace God's love and strive to walk the path toward holiness, however many times he might fall and get back up."

When the angel finished speaking, he took Jenna's hand and led her back a short distance from the Cross, where they could once again take in the whole scene of Calvary.

Jenna turned her attention to the Blessed Mother, standing at the foot of the Cross with a few others by her side. The angel pointed out the Apostle John and Mary Magdalene but reminded her that the rest had fled when Jesus was arrested. Jenna thought back to the crowds that hung on his words as he preached on the mountainside and the countless people he had healed. *Where had they all gone?*

Jesus looked at his mother standing by John, and said, "Woman, this is your son." Then to John, "This is your mother."

"In a final act of love and generosity," the angel said, "Jesus not only offered his whole life, but also gave his mother to all of humanity."

Jenna thought back to the Annunciation, the very first mystery that she prayed with the angel. Mary's assent to God's plan, and her unwavering faithfulness to it, carried her to this moment, where all could see how firm that "Yes" had been.

The time of Jesus' death was very close, so she returned her attention to the Cross. Jesus said, "I am thirsty," and the soldiers gave him some wine.

Then he said, "It is finished," and he died. To ensure that he was dead, a soldier thrust a lance into his side, and blood and water flowed out.

As they took Jesus' body down, his mother approached the soldiers, and they placed her Son in her arms. Unlike those early days, when Mary lovingly wrapped his body in swaddling clothes to protect him from the cold before placing him in the manger, she now held her Son's broken body, unable to protect him from his darkest hour.

Two men, whom the angel said were disciples of Jesus, came to bring his body to a tomb in a nearby garden, because the time of the Sabbath was nearing. The angel explained that, since no work could be done on the Sabbath, the full anointing for burial would have to wait until Sunday. Jenna and the angel followed the men, along with the women and John, to the garden. As she watched them place Jesus in the tomb, Jenna felt as though her heart was being buried with him.

After they left, Jenna and her angel sat in silence on a rock near the tomb looking up at the giant stone that covered its entrance. The knowledge of what was to come did not lessen the impact of that moment. Although Jenna knew the story of the Resurrection, she was still at Calvary.

The stone that stood between her and Jesus called to mind how she had often felt these past few years — that

God was absent. She had had so many questions, and yet God seemed to remain silent and still. Now, she still had questions, yet this time there was a glimmer of hope amid the obscurity. She now knew that God's silence wasn't because he didn't care. In fact, she had just witnessed how very much he does care. But she had to learn to wait for his answers to come in his time and in his way. The struggle to trust is real, but it is in the struggle that wisdom is given and faith is tested and purified.

Jenna and her angel sat motionless until evening fell on that first Good Friday. Then the angel prayed the Glory Be, gently breaking the long silence, and asked Jenna to conclude the mystery. She searched her heart, trying to put her deepest desire into words. She knew they would inevitably fall short, but she trusted that Jesus would understand her, anyway.

"Lord, help me to live my life, as Agnes did, in a way that is worthy of being your disciple. Help me to forgive like you and to love without reservation or condition. May your love fill me and inspire all that I do, especially the way I treat others, so that they might catch a glimpse in me of the love that you have for them."

Then the angel announced, with a hint of anticipation in his voice, "The first Glorious Mystery is The Resurrection."

The Glorious Mysteries

CHAPTER EIGHTEEN

The Resurrection

O happy fault, O necessary sin of Adam,
which gained for us so great a Redeemer!

Most blessed of all nights,
chosen by God to see Christ rising
from the dead!
Of this night scripture says:
'The night will be clear as day:
it will become my light, my joy.'

The power of this holy night
dispels all evil, washes guilt away,
restores lost innocence, brings
mourners joy;
it casts out hatred, brings us peace,
and humbles earthly pride
(From the Exultet).

171

A s they entered the Glorious Mysteries, dawn had broken on the first Easter Sunday. Jenna was still sitting with her angel in silence on a rock by the tomb where Jesus was buried, her heart heavy from all she had just witnessed. She noticed that the stone had been removed from the tomb.

Throughout this journey, Jenna had come to discover that Jesus was more than even the truest of friends. He was her brother and savior. As she watched the mysteries of her faith unfold before her eyes, she was discovering God's love in and around her.

This love, the very power that called her into existence, was speaking to the depths of her soul. She had rediscovered it like the memory of a precious secret long ago whispered in her ear, but somehow forgotten amidst the trials and confusion of life. Perhaps it had been stolen from her heart, or maybe she traded it for pleasures that deceptively promised to satisfy. But now, in the grace and power of that morning, this love, eternal yet brand new, burned brightly inside of her, and she vowed never to turn from it again. Rather, it would be the foundation for everything she did.

As she waited by the tomb, Jenna's whole being longed for what was about to take place. This event would not only impact the world, but she sensed that something profound was about to transpire within her soul, as well. Witnessing the Crucifixion left her heart feeling bruised and battered, but now the atmosphere around her felt fresh and clean, like the air after a thunderstorm. The change in the atmosphere seemed to be more than just a physical reality. She felt immersed in a healing energy that her heart and soul were absorbing like a sponge.

Jenna looked around to take in the new scene and noticed three women, whom she remembered from the foot of the Cross, heading somberly in her direction. They carried white, stone jars, which the angel told her contained spices to finish anointing Jesus' body. "They had been wondering how they would remove the stone that covered the entrance of the tomb," the angel said. "It was large and they had no plan, but their love and their faith drove them onward."

When the women arrived, they were surprised to see that the stone had already been moved away. Jenna followed the women as they entered the tomb looking for Jesus' body. Instead they saw an angel sitting to one side. A tangible joy radiated from him, and his clothes appeared dazzling white, matching the rosary in Jenna's hand. She waited in breathless anticipation for what would happen next.

As the angel spoke, his words carried within them the power of the miracle they announced. "Do not be afraid. You are looking for Jesus of Nazareth who was crucified, but he has been raised from the dead. See the place where he once lay. Go and tell his disciples and Peter, 'Jesus is going to Galilee. You will see him there.'"

A palpable joy rose from the depths of Jenna's soul, waking up her senses and causing her heart to soar. She looked toward the women with the spices and saw her joy reflected on their faces. They had arrived at the tomb crestfallen, with heavy steps, but they left with expressions full of wonder.

As they went to tell the apostles what they had just seen, to their surprise, Jesus himself appeared to them. Their eyes flew wide open. Jenna remembered their loyalty beneath the Cross and their sobs when his lifeless body was placed in his mother's arms. A part of them had surely died with him, but now he made all things new.

Jenna's angel, who had been standing close by, giving her just enough space, looked as though he could no longer contain himself. "Jesus' victory at the empty tomb reaches not only to the four corners of creation, but also into the deepest recesses of the human heart," he said. "Through his rising, he can also bring back to life the parts of your heart that have died from injury or sin. Just as he opened the tomb, he will open those places in your heart that you've closed off to the world, if you let him. It is not a promise that suffering will no longer come, but the assurance that it will never have the last word."

What the angel proposed would not always be easy. Some pain ran deep, and for that, she knew healing would take more time. The memories Jenna carried of Justin during his lowest points and the acute pain she still sometimes felt over her parents' divorce and the upheaval that followed, would all take time and grace to heal. Jenna knew it would be an ongoing struggle to place in God's hands that ever-present fear of losing Justin forever. However, she now saw more clearly than ever that, with God, all things are possible. If he could bring such good from the Cross, he could do the same with any situation.

Jenna stood motionless, wanting to hold onto that moment as long as possible. As she watched the women, her thoughts drifted back to the mystery of the Visitation, when Mary and Elizabeth alone shared the knowledge of Christ's Incarnation, and Jenna once again witnessed where true power lies. The prayers and faithfulness of the humble are what move the heart of God and draw from it his choicest blessings and most intimate secrets. It was through Mary's assent to God's plan that Jesus came into the world, and it was these faithful followers, who stood by him in his darkest hour, and now came to anoint his body, who would be the first disciples to announce his Resurrection, the most significant event in human history.

The women quickly found Peter and John and recounted everything they had seen. When the men heard the news, they ran to the tomb. As they saw for themselves that the tomb was empty, they let out a joyful cry. Undoubtedly, many questions would soon arise and many answers would come, but for now, in the splendor of that moment, they all faded into the background. Jenna looked over at her guardian angel, this time not in need of comfort, but with a desire to share with her loyal friend the intense joy that was so tangible in the air. Christ is risen! Not even death could contain him!

The Resurrection was now real to Jenna. Jesus was more than just another teacher — if he didn't rise from the dead, Christianity would make no sense. On the contrary, he conquered death, at work in every person, and broke the chains that hold us back from living life fully. God was not indifferent to evil and suffering; he had indeed responded, and this was his marvelous response: Christ was rejected that we might be reconciled to God; he was despised that we might know love; he suffered that we might be healed, and he died on a Cross that we might have life. Love was a Person, not an abstract concept, and not even death could overcome love. Rather, true love — the self-sacrificial kind revealed from the Cross — was the only force capable of conquering it. The Cross was now beautiful, not because of the anguish it represented, but because it was the instrument through which God chose to reveal the depths of his all-powerful love.

Jenna glanced over at her angel, close by her side, radiating the joy she felt. "Come, this is just the beginning. There is more to see in this mystery," he said, taking her hand. Then he placed his other hand on her shoulder, and she quickly closed her eyes, wondering where they would end up next.

***

The muffled sound of nearby conversations grew increasingly clear, and Jenna no longer felt the crisp morning air against her skin. She opened her eyes to find herself in a large room surrounded by Jesus' disciples. As she looked around, she realized it was the same room where the Last Supper took place. The angel informed her that it was now evening on the first Easter Sunday, and the disciples, still afraid for their lives because of their association with Jesus, remained behind locked doors.

With great anticipation, Jenna scanned the room, knowing she was about to witness another appearance of Jesus, and suddenly, to her great joy, there he was, standing in their midst. The angel gently squeezed Jenna's hand before letting go to allow her to turn her attention fully to the scene before her.

As Jesus appeared to his disciples for the first time, some stood breathless, while others stared incredulously at those around them. Some stepped back, away from where Jesus stood, and others shifted in place. Jenna could only imagine their guilt, knowing that all of the apostles, except John, had abandoned him in his time of need. Then she noticed Peter, the wonder in his expression mixed with agitation, and thought of his threefold denial just three days before. Jenna could imagine how afraid they must have been that all had been lost, but she had also witnessed Jesus' forgiveness from the Cross and knew he wouldn't hold a grudge.

The disciples looked intently at Jesus, waiting for him to speak. "Peace be with you," he said. His words did not condemn. Rather they seemed to impart on the disciples the peace of which he spoke. Their bodies relaxed, and joy made its way into their eyes. In some, there were tears of relief. Jenna, too, was consoled to see once again how quickly Jesus lets go of past mistakes.

Then he breathed on them, telling them to receive the Holy Spirit. "Whoever's sins you forgive will be forgiven and whoever's sins you retain will be retained." Jenna noticed that it was only after they had received forgiveness for their own betrayals that Jesus entrusted them with bringing his mercy to others. He seemed to be emphasizing that this was not a power to be lorded over others or offered haughtily.

The angel reminded Jenna that Thomas, one of the Twelve, was not in the room at that time, and that, when the disciples later recounted the story to him, he was not convinced. He insisted that, unless he touched the nail marks in Jesus' hands and feet, and the wound in his side, he would not believe. Jenna remembered the famous story and hoped she would see him receive that chance.

Then the angel motioned for her to follow him, and the two departed from the room. He brought her to a dusty country road leading away from Jerusalem, where they caught up with two of Jesus' disciples. As they slowed down to keep pace with the disciples, the angel informed her that they were headed for a village called Emmaus.

Jenna was listening to them discuss the events of the past few days when Jesus came up beside the disciples and began to walk with them. They did not appear to know it was he. When he asked what they were talking about, one of them gasped and said, "Could there be anyone in the area unaware of all that just happened?"

Then the disciple proceeded to explain that they were talking about the suffering and Crucifixion of Jesus of Nazareth, a mighty prophet whom they were hoping would be the one to redeem Israel. "It is the third day since this took place, and some women from our group said when they went to the tomb early this morning, his body was not there. Instead, there was an angel who announced Jesus was alive." Then his eyes widened as he said, "Some of us went to the tomb, and we found things just as the women had said."

Jesus replied, "Why are you so slow to understand? Don't you see how this is the fulfillment of all that the prophets spoke?! It was necessary that the Messiah suffer these things in order to conquer sin and death and redeem the world." Then he began to interpret for them all the passages that referred to him throughout all the Scriptures. They rubbed their chins as they listened to Jesus illuminate their sacred texts.

When the group arrived in Emmaus, the disciples invited him to stay the night, since it was almost dark. Later, while they were sharing a meal, Jesus took bread, said the blessing, broke it, and gave it to them. At that moment, just as recognition spread across their faces, he vanished from their sight.

"Were not our hearts on fire as he opened the Scriptures to us?" one of the disciples said. "Let's return at once to Jerusalem to tell the other disciples what happened and how Jesus revealed himself to us in the breaking of the bread."

Jenna, too, recognized "the breaking of the bread" as the ritual that Jesus had instituted at the Last Supper, and she realized she had just witnessed the Mass in its earliest form. After breaking open the Scriptures for his disciples, Jesus then broke bread with them, becoming so completely present in that act that he was able to disappear from their sight and still remain with them.

As she watched, Jenna felt a hunger, deep in her spirit, to receive the Lord in Holy Communion. With a rush of joy, she suddenly remembered that the next day was Christmas and told her angel she would find a way to get to Confession and attend Mass. Her first Communion in quite some time would take place on the feast of the

Nativity, when Christ became so small for her. "Now you are watching the mysteries of Christ's life unfold, but tomorrow at Mass, they will become part of you," her angel said, his eyes sparkling with anticipation.

Then, placing a gentle hand on Jenna's shoulder, he said, "Let's go back to the Upper Room."

***

A week had passed, he informed her as she opened her eyes, and the disciples were still behind locked doors. This time their conversation was more animated. Jenna noticed that Thomas was with them. She sympathized with him, because she knew how hard it was to believe based on another person's account, and after all, Thomas and the other apostles had staked everything on Jesus. She was excited that he would soon receive the assurance that can only come from an encounter with Jesus.

After a short time, Jesus again appeared in their midst and said, "Peace be with you."

Then he went over to Thomas. "Come, touch my hands and my side and do not doubt any longer, but believe in me."

"My Lord and my God!" Thomas said, his eyes wide with wonder.

Jesus looked at each of the disciples, then returned his gaze to Thomas. He leaned in and said, "You believe because you have seen with your own eyes, but blessed are all those who will come to believe in me without seeing."

A sense of warmth came over Jenna as she observed Jesus' patience with Thomas and with those who would later come to believe without the benefit of seeing. Her angel confirmed what she was beginning to understand.

"Jesus knew the apostles, the first bishops, would soon become spiritual fathers to many and that his rising from the dead, central to the Faith, would be challenging to accept. Over the course of his three years with them, Jesus had gradually revealed his identity and mission to his disciples, and he wanted to be sure they in turn were patient in their approach toward others. Facing their own weakness would prepare them to lead, with patience, those who would come to believe through their testimony." Jenna smiled. Jesus truly was the Good Shepherd who gives his loved ones enough light to see their weaknesses but bestows in abundance the grace necessary to overcome them.

While Jenna had watched the famous scene with Thomas, she was puzzled as to why Jesus' wounds were still present in his glorified state, if there wasn't supposed to be pain in Heaven. "Why didn't his wounds disappear when he rose from the dead?" she asked the angel.

The angel looked pleased at her observant question. "Jesus' life-giving wounds remained in his body as proof that love and mercy truly are the most powerful forces on

Earth." he said. "Christ did not eliminate suffering and death, but conquered them. He brought good from evil, life from death, and he continues to do the same every day in his Body, the Church. This can be trying, because the Cross is painful, but you can trust that it is possible because Christ has already won the battle between good and evil. This is the power of the Resurrection."

Jenna still wondered how Jesus would bring about good from her own problems. After all, her family was torn apart, her brother was missing, and her friend was gone. There was no going back. Yet her problems were small compared to the scene on Calvary. If God could bring good from the Cross, she had every reason to hope that he could do it through her suffering, too.

As Jenna stood amidst the disciples in the glory of the resurrected Christ, pondering all that she had just witnessed, time seemed to stand still, and the air felt heavy and dense. Even if she wanted to, she doubted she could move an inch. She knew with every fiber of her being that this encounter with Christ, a gift of Agnes' love, would forever change the course of her life.

The angel gave Jenna a short break before proceeding to the next scene. She sat in silence, leaning against a column in the Upper Room and giving her mind a rest from trying to absorb all that was happening in and around her. Then he told her that he wished to take her to another day, to the last of Jesus' appearances she would witness before the Ascension. When she felt the angel's hand on her shoulder, she closed her eyes.

***

She breathed in and, once again, felt the clean sea air fill her lungs. She opened her eyes to find herself back at the seashore, watching Peter and six others bring in their fishing boat. The morning sunlight was peaking over the horizon, bringing a hint of the splendid orange that would soon set the sky ablaze.

With shoulders slumped and eyes half closed they began the tiresome task of mending their empty nets. The scene reminded Jenna of that morning three years before when the disciples left everything behind to follow Jesus. Jesus was standing on the shore, but they did not seem to realize it was him.

"Cast your net over the right side of the boat."

They did as Jesus told them and caught so many fish that they were not able to bring in the nets.

John turned to Peter and shouted, "It is the Lord!" and Peter, barely clothed, jumped into the sea and swam ashore to meet him.

When all the disciples reached the shore, dragging the net filled with fish, they cooked some and had breakfast.

After they finished, Jesus asked Peter, "Do you love me more than these?"

"Yes, Lord, you know that I love you."

"Feed my lambs."

Jesus asked him again, "Do you love me?"

"Yes, Lord, you know that I love you."

"Tend my sheep."

Then Jesus asked a third time, "Do you love me?"

Peter looked down, shifting his weight back and forth. Then, looking straight at Jesus, his eyes moist, he said, "Lord, you know everything. You *know* that I love you."

"Feed my sheep." At these words a look of understanding broke across Peter's face, and he breathed a long sigh of relief. He had denied Jesus three times the night before he died and now he had been given the chance to make it right.

Warmth spread through Jenna's chest as she witnessed this tender encounter. After Peter's threefold denial of Jesus on the night before his Crucifixion, she remembered how distraught he was. She could only imagine the doubts he would have had about his ability to lead the Church. But even after such a painful betrayal in his hour of greatest need, Jesus didn't revoke the calling of the first pope. He not only forgave Peter, but he restored him. Now, with a profound new understanding of Jesus' mercy, Peter was finally ready to be the rock upon which Jesus would build his Church. If Jesus could forgive and restore Peter, there was hope for everyone. Maybe even Justin would go on to greatness.

Jenna could now see the Christian life for the great adventure that it was. She confided to the angel that she used to think Agnes' faith was merely a quaint part of her personality left over from another time. The angel smiled. "When you reach Heaven and see things through God's eyes, you may be surprised to learn who the real heroes are and where the most significant battles are fought."

Although she could still feel its power, Jenna sensed that the mystery was coming to a close. Hoping to prolong it, she asked her angel, "Are there other appearances of Jesus that we can go and see?"

"There would be no time to show you all of his appearances," he replied. "In the forty days after his Resurrection, Jesus taught them time after time and performed many beautiful signs. Heaven has shown you these, so that you might begin to understand the significance of this central event and your faith may increase."

So, with hands folded and head bowed, Jenna joined the angel in praying the Glory Be and offered her prayer to conclude the mystery. *"Lord Jesus, you have shown me that nothing I do can separate me from your love and that nothing is impossible for those who believe. Help me to remember this always and to open to you the parts of my heart that are wounded or dead through my own failings, so that the light of your Resurrection can shine brightly through them."*

Then the angel announced, "The second Glorious Mystery is The Ascension of the Lord."

CHAPTER NINETEEN

The Ascension

May the eyes of your hearts be enlightened, that you may know what is the hope that belongs to his call, what are the riches of glory in his inheritance among the holy ones, and what is the surpassing greatness of his power for us who believe, in accord with the exercise of his great might: which he worked in Christ, raising him from the dead and seating him at his right hand in the heavens, far above every principality, authority, power and dominion, and every name that is named not only in this age but also in the one to come. And he put all things beneath his feet and gave him as head over all things to the church, which is his body, the fullness of the one who fills all things in every way (Ephesians 1:18-23).

Feeling the angel's hand on her shoulder, Jenna closed her eyes and allowed the Our Father and Hail Marys they were praying to carry her into the second Glorious Mystery. Before long, she stood on a rocky hillside with the disciples, gathered around Jesus. The angel informed her it had been forty days since the Resurrection, and this would be their final encounter with Jesus before he returned to the Father.

"Over the course of his numerous appearances during the past forty days, Jesus had taught them about things they would not have understood before his Passion, Death, and Resurrection," the angel explained. "They now understood why he had to suffer and die before entering his glory."

The warmth of the sun was tapered by a cool, soothing breeze blowing through the crowd, abuzz with speculation at what would happen next. From the hillside, Jesus began to address the people in a loud voice, and a hush came over them. "Stay in Jerusalem until you are baptized with the Holy Spirit," he instructed.

They wondered aloud what this could mean and when it would take place, but there was no trace of doubt in their voices. After all, they had come to learn that what Jesus promised, he delivered. They discussed briefly among themselves how, before his death, Jesus had talked about returning to the Father so the Holy Spirit could come to them, but they did not press him for details. Jenna could understand how they might not want to think too much about his inevitable departure.

In a hopeful tone, one of the disciples asked, "Lord, when will you restore the kingdom of Israel?"

"The Father has determined this, but it is not for you to know," he said. "You are to stay in Jerusalem to receive power when the Holy Spirit comes upon you, so that you can be my witnesses throughout the world."

After Jesus spoke these parting words, he blessed them and was lifted up before their eyes towards the heavens. The disciples watched intently until a cloud blocked him from their view. Then, suddenly, two men in white appeared and said, "Why are you standing here looking up at the sky? Jesus, who has been taken up from you into Heaven, will return in the same way at the appointed time."

The sound of their voices startled Jenna, who also could not take her eyes off the spot where Jesus had vanished from their sight. She became lost in reflection as she tried to wrap her mind around the event she had just witnessed.

Jenna thought back to the previous mystery, when Jesus had appeared to the disciples in the days after the Resurrection. Jesus ate and drank with them, and the wounds from his Crucifixion had not disappeared. Now, as he ascended to Heaven, it was not just his spirit that rose up, but his body, as well. This meant that the marriage of divinity and humanity that took place at the Incarnation would forever remain. Jesus did not temporarily take on flesh, but he would always be fully God and fully man. This made her think of something

Agnes once said when Jenna asked how she could be so certain God understood her: "The heart of God is forever, in the Son, also the heart of a man."

This beautiful reality, which finally made sense to Jenna, was too much to take in. As with the Crucifixion, there was, indeed, no other way to begin to contemplate such a sublime mystery, except through the lens of the folly of God's love. Only such a love and desire for our happiness could explain the measures that God took to be with his children. *Such a God*, Jenna thought, *and he alone, is worthy of profound worship.*

Jenna's angel, ever faithfully at her side, was looking at her with tenderness. The gentle light that emanated from his eyes grew a little brighter, and the love that flowed forth from his gaze burrowed its way into her heart. "Jenna, even the angels are astonished at the manner in which God chose to redeem humanity," he said. "Even in Heaven you will never fully comprehend the mystery of his inexhaustible love, which perpetually seeks ways to pour itself out. In his divinity Jesus is eternally one with the Father, and in his humanity he has united himself with you. Jesus wants to draw you into their love, which is the Holy Spirit, whom he will soon pour out upon the disciples, so that his followers can share in the profound intimacy of the Trinitarian life.

"As promised," the angel continued, "Jesus will, indeed, come back at the end of time in the same manner in which he ascended, and he will judge the living and the dead. But you can rest assured that you will have a judge who understands your weakness and temptations and who loved you to the point of dying on a cross.

"Since Jesus died for every person, he alone has the right to pass judgment on a soul. Remember what he taught: For those who are merciful toward others, there will be mercy. For those who ignore the poor and the needs of others, there will be judgment. The way you treat others is the way you treat Christ himself." This reality was both comforting and frightening.

While she had been taught as a child that Jesus would one day return, Jenna was now learning that, in the meantime, he remained with his disciples in many real ways. He was different from other teachers, because he did not die and leave his followers alone to spread his message. Rather, he returned to the Father and would soon pour out his own Spirit upon his followers to teach, guide, and anoint with power their words and actions. God, who is perfect, would carry out his saving work down through the ages, through imperfect people.

There was no time to look toward the sky, no time for looking backwards at what was. It was time to move forward and onward. But first the disciples had to await the promised Holy Spirit, without whom they could do nothing.

Jenna realized how much her own life, too, was now caught up in the momentum of this mystery. Like the apostles, she could no longer go back to how things used to be. Whether she liked it or not, she was in a new school; her brother was still missing; her parents were no longer together, and Agnes was gone. But like the apostles, she, too, had encountered the Crucified and Risen One. It was time to move on and trust that, just as Jesus would equip the apostles for their mission in their world, he would not abandon her when she returned to her new world without Agnes.

With Jesus having ascended into Heaven and his promise of what was to come, Jenna was eager to accompany the disciples back to Jerusalem, where the Church would be born and their mission would begin. Her heart filled with gratitude, Jenna and the angel prayed the Glory Be, and she once again brought the mystery to a close, as the angel had taught her, with a prayer from her heart.

"Lord, thank you for all you did for us — for taking on our humanity forever at the Incarnation, for the years you spent teaching, for your Passion, Death, and Resurrection, and for ascending into Heaven to open the way for us. Continue to open my eyes to all the ways that you remain present in our midst."

After Jenna's heartfelt prayer, the angel announced, "The third Glorious Mystery is The Descent of the Holy Spirit."

CHAPTER TWENTY

The Descent
of the Holy Spirit

Among human beings, who knows what pertains to a person except the spirit of the person that is within? Similarly, no one knows what pertains to God except the Spirit of God. We have not received the spirit of the world but the Spirit that is from God, so that we may understand the things freely given us by God. And we speak about them not with words taught by human wisdom, but with words taught by the Spirit, describing spiritual realities in spiritual terms (1 Corinthians 2:11-13).

As the angel removed his hand from Jenna's shoulder and she opened her eyes, they were back in the Upper Room, once again in the midst of the disciples, and Mary was with them. They were one hundred and twenty all together, and the doors were locked, because they were still afraid of being arrested for their connection with Jesus, her angel said, filling in some details of the event. Nine days had passed since the Ascension, and they remained together, as Jesus had instructed, praying for the Holy Spirit.

Suddenly, while they were praying, a noise like a rushing wind came from above and filled the entire house. Tongues of fire appeared and rested above each of their heads. Jenna had learned about Pentecost, the birthday of the Church, in her Confirmation program, but back then she had been doubtful that it actually happened this way. She thought it sounded more like an exaggerated story than an historical event. Yet here she was, spellbound, watching as the Spirit of God descended upon every person in the room.

As the Holy Spirit came upon them, they began praising God with all their might, speaking with great fervor of his wondrous works and his faithful love. Their voices resounded through the room. They were loud yet harmonious, like a symphony with many different parts working together to form something even more beautiful than its individual pieces. There was a unity apparent even amidst so much activity and diversity.

Jenna slowly scanned the room, wanting to take in the entire scene before her. Many of the disciples were praying in different languages. Some relayed visions, while others prophesied, speaking out words that they believed the Lord was prompting them to say. Some appeared overjoyed as they tasted the sweetness of God, while others, awestruck, remained still. Some had an expression of clarity on their faces, as if a light was turned on in their mind and they finally understood things that had previously eluded them. And an indescribable joy permeated the scene, like the glue holding it all together.

It was not hot, but the air felt so thick that Jenna could barely move. Her angel explained that the heaviness she experienced was another manifestation of God's presence around them.

More than simply witnessing what was taking place, she could feel inside her the sweet effects of the Spirit. She felt a love for God deep within that seemed insatiable, and a bold confidence came upon her. In that moment, Jenna could think of nothing more important than for every person to know their Creator and his immense love for them. She had been taught in religious education classes that she had received the Holy Spirit at Baptism and Confirmation, but now she was experiencing that reality. For the first time it all felt real.

As she continued to watch the event unfold, Jenna became aware that she was able to perceive more than her eyes alone could see. A gentle light spread across her mind, illuminating the scene before her. While all the disciples were sharing a common experience, it was also deeply personal for each one. The Spirit was pouring himself into the depths of every soul, bringing the grace and the gifts best suited for each one. As water finds its way into every crack and crevice of a vessel, the Holy Spirit, the Living Water, was making his way into those broken areas of their hearts, bringing healing to their interior wounds, filling their voids, and breaking the chains of sin that held them in bondage.

A visible change, evident in their expressions, was taking place in the men and women in the Upper Room that wondrous morning. The angel, who appeared to be in his element, provided deeper insight. "Jenna, you are witnessing the Holy Spirit bestowing, as he sees fit for each one, various grace and spiritual gifts to build them up, both individually and as a community. God is restoring to his children the happiness and wholeness he had always intended for them, but of which sin had robbed them. He is filling their weakness with strength, replacing their shame with his unconditional love, their fear with boldness, and exchanging their weariness for joy." The Holy Spirit was not some abstract concept or nebulous force. He was a Person whose presence was having real and visible affects so beautiful that no words could capture them.

As Jenna looked out upon the one hundred and twenty, she suddenly realized that her own faith had come to her, down through so many generations, from the witness of someone right there in that room, someone who, just moments before, was hiding in fear. She expressed to her angel how truly astounding it was that God can work so powerfully through imperfect people.

The angel smiled. "When God looks at his children, he sees in them their true potential, the person he created them to be. He heals and transforms them into men and women who intimately know his love and mercy, then sends them out to set the world ablaze.

"God desires people's free cooperation in his creative work so much that he trusts weak human beings who make mistakes — sometimes grave and costly mistakes. Yet this has always been his way. As God entrusts an innocent baby to its parents, so, too, does he entrust you to one another in so many beautiful ways, continually working through fragile human beings — family members, bishops and priests, teachers, friends — to transmit to every generation his truth and grace."

The angel's words helped crystalize in Jenna's mind the importance of pardoning others for their failings, especially if she wanted to be pardoned for hers. After all, everybody makes mistakes, and everybody needs forgiveness.

Jenna turned her attention towards Jesus' mother, naturally present on the birthday of the Church. She appeared radiant as she witnessed yet another of God's miracles. Jenna recalled the first time the Holy Spirit had descended upon her, at the Annunciation, when he overshadowed her and Jesus was conceived in her womb.

As though he knew where her thoughts had drifted, the angel observed, "At the Annunciation, Mary became the mother of Jesus, but now on Pentecost, Mary's motherhood takes on new meaning. As the mother of the Church, she will nurture and guide the infant Church, the Body of Christ her Son. As Jesus took flesh in her through the power of the Holy Spirit, so, too, will the members of Christ's Body, the Church, be formed by the Holy Spirit under her prayerful and maternal care. "

The two stood in silence as Jenna gazed around the room and continued to process all she was seeing and hearing. After some time, her angel placed his hand on her shoulder, bowed his head, and thanked God, with a voice full of promise, for so many blessings bestowed upon his young charge. Then he looked thoughtfully at Jenna and said, "There is so much I want to teach you right now, Jenna, but the Spirit himself will gradually instruct you in the years to come. As you continue to open your heart to him, he will draw you more deeply into his love and plan for your life. This is only the beginning for you.

"God's Spirit is always present to bring you the grace you need at every moment," he continued. "The mighty wind you heard blowing through this house is the same wind that came across the shapeless mass of creation in the Book of Genesis and formed it into the earth, and it is this same Spirit that raised Jesus from the dead.

At Baptism and Confirmation, the same Holy Spirit came upon you, as well, and he will continue to recreate you to the degree that you trust him. He wants to raise up the parts of you that are weak and wounded and bring back to life the places in your heart that are dead from sin and past injuries, so that you can love and live more fully. The only thing that can stop him is your refusal to cooperate with his grace. It is only by holding on to bitterness, pride, anger, and unhealthy behaviors that you can block his blessings."

Jenna turned her attention back to the disciples. Now that they had tasted the grace and power of the Holy Spirit, their focus turned outward. It was not enough to bask in the glory of the moment. There seemed to be a fire burning in them that was stronger than the fears that previously caused them to hide.

Pentecost was a Jewish feast celebrating the first fruits of the harvest and the giving of the Law to Moses on Mt. Sinai, the angel told Jenna. This meant that devout Jews had come to Jerusalem from every nation to celebrate the feast, and, upon hearing the sounds coming from the house where the disciples were staying, a large crowd gathered outside. They asked, "If all these people are Galileans, how is it that we each hear them in our own native language?" Some of them even accused the disciples of being drunk.

Peter arose with the other apostles and addressed them in a bold, confident voice. "These people are not drunk. It is only nine o'clock in the morning. Rather, this is what God was referring to when he said through the prophet Joel, 'In the last days, I will pour out a portion of my spirit upon all people. Some will prophesy, others will see visions, and yet others will dream dreams.'"

Peter boldly continued, "God worked through Jesus of Nazareth to perform signs and miracles in your midst, as you yourselves know. You had him crucified, but God raised him from the dead, because death could not hold him." Peter then proceeded to bring to light the Scriptures pertaining to Jesus.

"What should we do, my brothers?" one of the men asked.

"Turn from your sin and be baptized, so that your transgressions will be forgiven, and you will receive the gift of the Holy Spirit, just as we have."

Jenna stared intently at the scene, awestruck at the transformation that took place in the disciples. After Jesus' arrest, most of them had fled, and, even just a few hours before, had been hiding in fear of the authorities. But when the Holy Spirit came, everything changed. And Jenna was confident that he would remain with her, too, even after this experience with her angel came to a close and she returned to everyday life. The Holy Spirit would be with her to help her overcome her own personal struggles and to live and love as Jesus taught.

"About three thousand became disciples that day," the angel said. "In the time to come, the disciples would grow in number and continue to preach the Gospel with signs and wonders accompanying their words. They would endure great persecution, and eventually all the apostles, except John, would be martyred. But the faith would spread to the four corners of the world."

As the scene ended the angel led her in the Glory Be. Then she prayed, *"Holy Spirit, who raised Jesus from the dead, come into my heart and into my life, and fill every part of me with your presence. Heal me, guide me, strengthen me, and help me to be open every day to your inspirations."*

Then she looked over at her trusted friend, who announced, "The fourth Glorious Mystery is The Assumption of Mary."

CHAPTER TWENTY-ONE

The Assumption of Mary

If the Spirit of him who raised Jesus from the dead dwells in you then he who raised Jesus from the dead will bring your mortal bodies to life also through his Spirit dwelling in you (Romans 8.11).

As they prayed the Our Father and Hail Marys, Jenna felt her angel's hand resting on her shoulder and closed her eyes, curious where they would go next. When her eyes opened, she found herself in a new and unfamiliar place, so she was glad to have the angel fill in some of the details of the scene they had entered.

"Many years had passed since the birth of the Church on that first Pentecost, and Mary's life on Earth was coming to a close. Her life's work was nearing completion, and it was at long last time for her to be reunited with her Son in Heaven.

"God had kept her in the world for a time to help teach and guide the infant Church. He had chosen her to be the mother of his Son, and he wanted no less for the Church in those early years. But soon he would call her home. The longing in her heart to be with God surpassed every other desire. The moment for God to take her to her unique place in Heaven as daughter to the Father, mother to the Son, and spouse to the Holy Spirit, had, at long last, arrived."

There was a profound stillness to the scene. Jenna gazed upon Mary for a long time. She thought back to the first time she saw her at the Annunciation, where Jenna's journey began. Mary was much older now, yet Jenna thought she looked more beautiful than ever. Along with the purity that seemed to permeate her whole being, her faith and wisdom had attained full maturity over the course of a lifetime of faithfully following God's will, even to the foot of the Cross. The love that burned in her eyes as a young girl had been tried in fire and found true. Her faith had been challenged to the core and proven to be rock solid.

Then came the thirty years Mary had spent living with Jesus in the quiet of Nazareth, where she and Joseph had made a home for him. Jenna thought about the intimacy they knew — sharing the joys, sorrows, and struggles of everyday life. Daily, Mary heard the very Word of God speak to her, and she pondered in her heart the mysteries of life with the Son of God.

Later, Mary followed her Son's public ministry with the concern of a mother and the attentiveness of a faithful disciple. A few years after his ministry began, with unspeakable sorrow she stood by him during his Passion and Death, absorbing in her heart every insult and every blow he endured. Knowing her Son like no other, she would have understood better than anyone the full cost of every rejection and every jeer. Yet even in her grief, as the Roman soldier placed the bruised and bloodied body of her Son in her arms, she never wavered. On that first Easter Sunday, her trust was rewarded beyond all imaginings when she saw anew the realization of the angel's promise at the Annunciation, that nothing would be impossible for God.

Then at Pentecost she witnessed God's saving plan coming to fruition. The same Spirit that had overshadowed her so long ago was poured out upon every disciple. In those early days of the Church, she was there for the first Christians, guiding, praying, teaching, and loving them because Jesus, truly giving everything he had to his disciples, entrusted them to her maternal care from the Cross. And now that her mission in the world was complete, it was time for her long-awaited reunion with Jesus.

Knowing that Jenna was about to witness an event that would be difficult to comprehend, her angel provided her with some background. "Mary was conceived without sin," he explained. "Therefore, her body would not be subjected to decay at the end of her earthly life. She would experience the fullness of redemption as soon as her life on Earth came to a close. Mary was granted this singular grace based on the anticipated merits of her Son's eternal victory.

"Being the mother of Jesus, Mary was, therefore, the Mother of God, the pure vessel from which Christ took his entire humanity. Jesus honored his mother with the best gift he could give her — he kept her untouched by sin from the moment of conception. And she remained so pure her entire life that the enemy could not win even the slightest victory over her. Since death is the ultimate fruit of sin, when her time came, she was taken into Heaven body and soul, without having to wait until the end of time for the redemption of her body."

Jenna reflected for some time on the angel's words, trying her best to understand. She looked at Mary, whose joy mounted as her time drew near, then at the disciples, with mixed emotions on their faces. She imagined that Mary's departure would be bittersweet for the first disciples. They would certainly be grief-stricken when she left, but they also must have shared her joy in knowing that she would soon be reunited with Jesus.

The angel stood close to Jenna, his attention also fixed upon Mary and the disciples. "She was a true mother to them," he said. "From the beginning, when her 'Yes' made the Incarnation possible, to the end of her earthly life, she had given herself completely to God's saving plan. She was a source of tremendous comfort after Jesus ascended to the Father, standing as a beautiful sign of God's provision for his children. Those who knew Jesus while he walked the Earth could still see his features upon her countenance, and those who never met him could almost see him through her.

"She tirelessly recounted stories of Jesus' early years, providing valuable information that would later be recorded in the four gospel accounts. Her wisdom and prayers helped guide the apostles, who would pass on the Faith to all generations. They spent hours in her presence, where she would patiently teach the same lessons, over and over, continually calling them to prayer, penance, and renunciation of sin, and reminding them of the great love of God. Her departure was a sign that the Gospel had taken root and the Church was growing strong, and now it was time to continue her maternal role from the glory of Heaven. Like Jesus, she would always be with them, but in a new way."

Jenna looked down at the rosary in her hand. This timeless prayer was yet another way that Mary continued to teach her children about the Life, Death, and Resurrection of her Son. For generations, countless Christians, including Agnes, have entrusted themselves to Mary's prayers and wisdom, and as a result, have fallen ever more deeply in love with her Son.

When Mary's time had come, the apostles and disciples were gathered around her. Jenna stood nearby, arm in arm with her angel, taking in the whole scene. The love in Mary's heart was spilling over as she praised and glorified God. She was a model for Christians to the end.

Her spiritual children continued singing hymns, while Mary fell silent. Their love for her and for God poured forth through their voices and filled the room. After some time, a profound silence fell upon them. Mary closed her eyes and took her last breath. The apostles carried her body, solemnly and with tender care, to a nearby tomb.

***

The angel informed Jenna that three days had passed. They were again at Mary's tomb, where the apostles and a large number of disciples were gathering to pray. But when they arrived, they found that her body was no longer there. On impulse, they looked up toward the sky where they saw Heaven opening and the Blessed Virgin Mary being taken up by angels, who were singing a sweet melody. The joy in the air was tangible, along with a sense of long-awaited victory. Jenna stared at the sky for several minutes, unable to look away, then turned toward her guardian angel, hoping for an explanation.

The angel looked at Jenna with profound respect. "Mary's Assumption is not simply for her alone. It is also a sign of your own future in Christ," he said. "At the Last Judgment, when your body and soul are reunited, your redemption, like Mary's, will be complete. This happened immediately for Mary, because she was untouched by sin. She was the first Christian to believe at the Annunciation, and she is the first Christian to experience every fruit of Christ's redemptive work. It is a mother's privilege to go before her children in all things, and Mary's Assumption points to the future glorification for which every person is destined."

Jenna's heart overflowed with awe and gratitude for all Jesus had done, even to sharing his own mother. Like scenes from a movie, images from his Incarnation and Birth, his tireless preaching and healing, his Passion, Death, and Resurrection, and finally his Ascension and the pouring out of his Spirit, flashed through her mind. When she prayed the Glory Be with her angel, Jenna put her whole heart into it, feeling as though it was impossible to ever say those words adequately.

As she began her prayer to close the mystery, she knelt down at the tomb of Mary and opened her heart to her mother in Heaven. *"Blessed Mother, please pray for me and teach me to love God the way you did, by giving myself completely to him and trusting in his plan for me. I pray, too, for the grace to accept in peace my own inevitable death, whenever that may be, knowing it will bring me to the joy of Heaven, for which I was made."*

When she finished, Jenna suddenly realized she was about to enter the final mystery of the Holy Rosary. Sadness briefly came over her at this thought, but before it could settle in, her eyes were drawn back to the sky to that beautiful scene of Mary entering Heaven, which was still taking place before her.

When Jenna stood up, she noticed there were angels all around her. A sweet peace overtook her senses, and a breeze carried the scent of roses. As the next mystery unfolded before their eyes, the angel quickly announced, "The fifth Glorious Mystery is The Coronation of Mary."

CHAPTER TWENTY-TWO

The Coronation
of Mary

Then God's temple in heaven was opened, and the ark of his covenant could be seen in the temple. There were flashes of lightning, rumblings, and peals of thunder, an earthquake, and a violent hailstorm. A great sign appeared in the sky, a woman clothed with the sun, with the moon under her feet, and on her head a crown of twelve stars (Revelation 11:19-12:6a).

Mary was taken up to Heaven, while Jenna and her guardian angel stood with the disciples looking up. As Mary approached the heavens, surrounded by angels singing and praising God, the sky opened, and Jenna caught a brief glimpse of the next world.

She saw a crown being placed upon Mary's head, although she could not see the One who placed it there.

Even through that small opening in the sky, it was evident that Heaven had been eagerly awaiting her arrival. "After all," the angel pointed out, "as the King's mother, she is Heaven's Queen." A celebration and rejoicing broke out in Heaven, the likes of which Jenna could never have imagined. The Blessed Mother could not contain her joy at finally being with God, and that joy seemed to overflow into the hearts of everyone Jenna could see, as they magnified God for his wondrous works.

Jenna's heart soared as she saw for herself that Heaven does exist and its inhabitants are immersed in God's eternal love, which Agnes once told her was the joy and wholeness for which every human heart is made. Although she was limited in how much of Heaven she was able to see, she knew with every fiber of her being that it was a place she longed to be.

As Jenna contemplated these events, her eyes were drawn to her angel, who was also looking up toward Heaven. She saw on his face a renewed peace as he gazed toward his home, and she longed to possess his deep familiarity with the supernatural, which he seemed to take for granted.

As if feeling her stare, he turned his attention back to Jenna. He could not seem to stop himself from talking about his Queen.

"Do not let the honors bestowed upon her scare you," he said. "Even in her royalty, Mary exercises her role in a maternal fashion. From Heaven she tirelessly intercedes for the good intentions and well-being of her children with the effectiveness she had at Cana, because Jesus cannot say 'no' to the woman who bore him in her womb and loved him throughout his life into his darkest hour.

"Mary longs to see the Body of Christ, the Church, come to full stature and be with her in the glory of Heaven. She loves you beyond all telling. She sees all that God created you to be and wants nothing less than your truest potential to be realized.

"Jenna, Mary cares for you just as she cared for Jesus," he said. "When you are lost, like Jesus as a Boy in the Temple, she searches for you until you are back safely in her maternal embrace. She will teach you to love him with the purity of heart that she possesses and impart her gentle spirit upon you. It is through Mary that Jesus came into the world, and she is the safest way back to him. He loves when you come to him through his mother," the angel assured her. "Like any relationship, your relationship with God takes two, and who better than Mary to teach you your part?"

Jenna recalled Mary's words to Elizabeth at the Visitation, when she foretold that all generations would call Mary blessed. She was struck by the realization that she, too, would be part of the multitude that, through the ages, fulfilled this prophetic word. She felt united to all those, including Agnes, who faithfully prayed the Rosary and proclaimed to Mary many times every day, "Blessed are you among women."

She looked back toward the sky that had parted to receive the Blessed Mother. Slowly, the opening in the sky widened, and, for a moment Jenna saw multitudes of angels and saints. Suddenly, they were all around her, with their strength and prayers. They seemed to be cheering her on. Then she saw Our Lady, wearing a golden crown, standing in front of a bright light. Mary gazed down upon her with a look of love that set her heart ablaze. Joy flooded Jenna's entire being at the knowledge of so much love and of belonging to something so beautiful as the family of God.

After a few moments, Jenna could no longer see them, but she still felt their presence. "Every time you recall in prayer these mysteries of faith," the angel said, "you enter eternity and bring Heaven to Earth. In these moments, whether you perceive it or not, all of Heaven is with you, including Agnes and all your loved ones who have gone before you. The veil is so much thinner than you can imagine, Jenna."

Jenna couldn't help but wonder why she had been so blessed to be taken on this great adventure through the Gospel. So she asked her angel, "Why was I granted this privilege when there are so many others on the planet more deserving than me? Why was *I* given this extraordinary experience?"

The angel paused and looked down, as if carefully choosing his words. "God's love is infinite, and so he loves you as if you are the only person in the world. Every soul has its moments of grace, but the reasons for God's unique ways with each one often remain a mystery until they meet him face to face.

"However, you can rest assured, Jenna, that God is always at work in everyone's life to draw each person to himself. If people knew how loved they were, the world would be a different place, because they would always try to love others as God loves them.

"Jesus overcame death, so that you could be with him forever, and he counts on those who know him to bring his saving love to those who do not. More often than you can imagine, Jenna, great graces are granted through the prayers and quiet witness of heroes like Agnes."

Jenna was aware that this unforgettable experience of the Rosary was nearing its end, so she took a few moments to prepare herself to return to the world she knew. As the small opening that still remained in the heavens closed back up, Jenna sat on the ground with her legs crossed and bowed her head. The air around her felt dense, as if a heavy blanket rested upon her shoulders, and she reflected on her experience. She thought about how important Agnes had been in her life. She was a beacon, a wise and faithful friend during difficult times. But now

Jenna understood just how precious a soul like Agnes was in God's eyes, as well.

The angel discreetly sat next to his young friend in the same manner. As Jenna thought about returning to everyday life, her thoughts went back to Mary. Most of her days on Earth had been filled with the ordinary tasks of family life. Yet she lived the mysteries of the Gospel and pondered them daily. She did not always understand what God was asking of her, but she accepted God's will with heroic faith and love, no matter what the personal cost. Jenna thought in amazement about the ultimate end to which that led her.

"This is where a wholehearted 'yes' to God will lead," the angel said softly, as if reading her thoughts. "The more you surrender to God, the more beautifully he will act in your life. The greatest saints are the ones who held nothing back from him. They took him at his word and staked everything on his promises.

"Jesus brought you and Agnes together, and he was by your side the night she died, the night you thought you lost your beloved friend forever," he continued. "Agnes is alive forever in Jesus, but he also wants you to understand that he gave you his mother at the Cross. The Rosary is Mary's prayer. These are the mysteries she pondered throughout her whole life, and she wants you to do the same so that you will grow in love for her Son.

"Throughout your life, as you remain faithful to this prayer, she will open to you the treasures of her heart, as mothers do for their children. Now you can visit Mary through the Rosary the way you used to visit Agnes, and she will guide you as you discern your vocation, your mission, and discover all the gifts that God has bestowed upon you for your benefit and for the benefit of all those whose lives yours will touch."

When the angel finished speaking, he stood up. Jenna followed him, placing her hand in his out-stretched hand. They prayed the last Glory Be, looking toward the heavens, and Jenna began her prayer that would conclude the twentieth and final mystery of the most holy Rosary.

"Mary, you are my heavenly Mother, and Jesus gave us to one another from the Cross. I promise to make this prayer a part of my daily life. Please open to me all the riches of this beautiful prayer in the days and months and years to come. You pondered these mysteries in your heart during your life on Earth, and allowed each one of them to take root in your soul and bear unimaginable fruit. Teach me to walk in God's ways and always to remember that my true home is with God in Heaven."

CHAPTER TWENTY-THREE

Concluding Prayers

I came so that they might have life and have it more abundantly (John 10:10).

Jenna's angel then led her toward a nearby winding road, where they would conclude their prayer. They walked together like two old friends lingering after a visit, not wanting to leave one another's company. Jenna had grown to love her guardian angel, and her angel confided how overjoyed he was at having the opportunity to communicate so directly with his precious young charge.

While the angel led Jenna in the Hail, Holy Queen and the Rosary Prayer (the concluding prayers of the Rosary) Jenna bowed her head and listened intently to the words, since she did not yet know these prayers by heart. Then they ended by making the Sign of the Cross.

The two continued walking. Jenna was absorbed in silence, trying to prepare herself for her angel's inevitable departure. As she anticipated the angel leaving, she became fearful. "What if I forget everything I have just learned? What if it all fades away when I can no longer see and hear you?"

The angel looked compassionately at Jenna, giving her a reassuring smile. "Be at peace, Jenna. God has more ways than you could ever imagine of communicating with a soul.

"You have just witnessed all that Jesus did to be close to you and to share your joys and trials. Trust in the promise he made before ascending to the Father — that he would be with you always. There are times you will feel his presence with your senses, and other times his Spirit will come upon you quietly, without detection, and communicate directly with your own spirit. In those times you will see him by the fruit his visits bear in your life. Trust that God always knows what you need even better than you do, Jenna.

"When you pray the Rosary each day, it will not always be a dramatic experience. There will be Rosaries that bring great consolations, and others will feel as dry as the desert. Each mystery is like a multifaceted diamond that can be contemplated from many angles. If you persevere, you will grow with the mysteries, and they will grow with you."

They continued walking. "There is so much more for you to learn. You are at the beginning of a great adventure. There will be doubts and challenges, but you will continue to grow through prayer, study, and life experience. Keep asking life's tough questions, Jenna, as you always have. God will bring the right people into your life to instruct you, and he will teach you in ways you can't yet imagine," he promised. "And I am never far. Even when you can't perceive me with your senses, I am close by, protecting, guiding, and praying for you."

Jenna knew all along that there was so much in these mysteries that she couldn't yet grasp. At times, the knowledge revealed seemed to wash right over her before her mind could take hold of it. However, it reassured her to know that she had a lifetime to go back and mine those treasures.

"There are so many more things I could have explained to you," the angel said. "We only touched the surface tonight, but you were given exactly what you needed at this time in your journey. When you come back to these mysteries in your mind, sit with Mary in Nazareth; hold the baby Jesus in the stable; take Jesus by the hand as a child your age and pour out your heart to him; kneel at the foot of the Cross; ask for the Holy Spirit as you meditate upon that first Pentecost.

"Like the first Christians, Jenna, you, too, are now a witness to the power of the Gospel. The thin veil separating time and eternity was lifted for you. Allow it to transform you, because a spiritual experience is only as good as the fruit it produces."

As she walked the final leg of her journey, Jenna began to think with deep regret about the anger at God she had carried for so long, and her lack of trust in him. She knew now he had always been with her, and her failings were not for lack of his provision.

As if sensing her peace was disturbed, the angel quickly drew her attention off of her own weakness and back to God's great love. "God understands your shortcomings, Jenna, and is eager to forget every transgression. Make frequent use of the Sacraments to obtain his peace, which surpasses understanding," he said, with great optimism in his voice.

"The Church contains every grace you could possibly need, and they are available to you in abundance. Never doubt God's desire to forgive everything and embrace you as often as you turn back to him, whether your transgression is large or small. Even if you should forget everything else, Jenna, always remember that no sin is greater than the mercy of God."

Jenna was aware that she had been given an incredible gift. She had tasted God's love and was convinced that her response had to be more than words. From now on, every action and decision would be her response, so that one day her very life would cry back to God, "I love you, too!"

Knowing their time left together was short, Jenna was holding fast to each word the angel spoke and soaking in the peace that radiated from his being. The angel treated her with a dignity she had often tasted in her encounters with Agnes. She knew this would be a feeling she would return to often in her thoughts, when the world made her feel unimportant. She would always remember how respected and loved she felt in the angel's presence, and would never again permit anyone to let her feel otherwise.

As their walk came to an end, the angel turned to Jenna, and, taking both of her hands in his own, he looked intently into her eyes. His expression was full of hope and promise. "Jenna, even though you will not see me much longer, I will always be at your side, sharing your joys and sorrows, as your life unfolds and the graces received from this experience take root in your life. Then, some day, known only to God, I will escort you to Heaven." Jenna's heart leapt at the thought of that moment. That alone was reason enough to persevere.

As the moment drew to a close, he added, "Jenna, do not limit God, but allow him free reign in your heart, and he will make your life more beautiful than the most exquisite work of art. Your plans for your life could never be as wonderful as what God has in mind for you. His love for you is infinite and his only limitations are those that you place on him. Entrust yourself completely to God and to his designs and let him surprise you with a life that will surpass your wildest dreams."

When the angel finished speaking, Jenna closed her eyes. She prayed she would always do as the angel taught and surrender everything to God, who was worthy of all her trust.

CHAPTER TWENTY-FOUR

Conclusion

Therefore, since we are surrounded by so great a cloud of witnesses, let us rid ourselves of every burden and sin that clings to us and persevere in running the race that lies before us... (Hebrews 12:1).

When Jenna opened her eyes, she found herself back in her living room facing the Christmas tree. Her angel was still with her, sitting next to the tree, in the same spot where he first appeared. Jenna was not surprised when she looked down and saw that the rosary she had been praying with was no longer in her hands. She knew it had only been borrowed. Jenna's rosary was the one under the tree in the box that Agnes had wrapped. The angel made a gesture towards Agnes' gift, and Jenna knew the moment to open it had arrived.

She slowly unwrapped the box and carefully took Agnes' rosary into her hands. She held it like a rare treasure entrusted to her by the beloved daughter of a great Queen. It was worn out, beaten up, and faded. Some of the beads were scratched, others were chipped, but each imperfection was precious to Jenna, because it represented countless years of heartfelt prayer and heroic faith in God's providence. The battle-worn rosary was a silent witness to Agnes' fidelity and childlike trust in God, and woven into each bead were the joys and sorrows of a lifetime.

Jenna wondered how many people Agnes had carried straight to the heart of God through her prayers. How many chains of fear and anger, addiction and selfishness, which keep the human heart in bondage, had been broken through prayers said on the rosary Jenna was holding? And how many more miracles would be obtained through Jenna's own prayers?

Like a mighty weapon in the hand of a great warrior, she knew that Agnes had defeated countless enemies with that rosary in hand. Like David, whose faith and slingshot defeated Goliath, Agnes, too, came up victoriously against so many giants, so many seemingly impossible situations in her life. The love and trust with which Agnes had prayed that rosary proved time and time again to be a sure key to the treasures of the Lord's heart.

Jenna thought about how she would follow in the footsteps of so many great men and women by taking up this prayer. She was eager to carry into her own generation the torch that Agnes had passed her. She could think of so many people for whom she longed to pray, people in need of grace and hope, and all the challenges in her own life that she would entrust to its power.

She would begin by praying for Justin, who desperately needed God's protection and mercy, and for her parents, that they, too, might experience God's healing and peace. She also thought of Maggie and other friends. She would carry them all in her heart each day as she prayed the Rosary.

Jenna now possessed deeper insight into Agnes' ways. Her wisdom, which had always attracted Jenna, now burned even more brightly in her memory, because Jenna finally understood its source. Jenna had a deeper appreciation of her friend who, over the years, had become conformed to these mysteries, breathing them in until they animated her whole being. Every day with her rosary in hand, Agnes meditated upon the inexhaustible mysteries of the Gospel, with Mary as her guide, opening her heart to the transforming power contained in them, and never shying away from the hard work of conversion.

In Agnes, Jenna knew she had a beautiful model of a woman who tried every day to live out those mysteries, drawing upon herself, and the whole world, the riches of the Gospel. She understood now that Agnes' eyes did, indeed, contain the fountain of youth, for the Holy Spirit, who is the source of all life, shined through them. She was beginning to grasp that secret she sometimes felt Agnes longed to impart: All the love put together that we experience throughout our entire lifetime is only a pale reflection of God's love for us, and this infinite love of God can never be taken from us.

As she reflected, Jenna glanced down into the gift box and noticed a small card she hadn't seen before. Her heart leapt as she recognized Agnes' handwriting.

My Dearest Jenna,

Please accept this gift that comes to you with all the love in my heart and with so many prayers offered for your happiness. My beloved young friend, may the Rosary keep us always united, but more importantly, may it be your gateway to Heaven, as it has been mine, and your key to life's most beautiful treasures.

Love always,

Agnes

As Jenna read Agnes' parting words to her, her eyes filled with tears. It seemed as though her friend were right beside her. She sensed that Agnes had been with her throughout this whole experience, offering her love and her friendship each step along the way. However, it was more than Agnes' presence alone that she felt. Throughout the Rosary, Jenna sensed that she and the angel were never alone. Somewhere in the background was a silent multitude journeying with them and strengthening Jenna with its prayers and its presence.

Jenna's angel, who had remained silent since they returned to her living room, spoke to her for the last time. She looked intently at him, knowing it would be her last chance to impress his image into her memory.

"Indeed, Jenna, you are never alone when you come to these mysteries. The Church, past, present, and future, converges at each one, where time and eternity meet. And those whom you carry in your heart are also present in a mysterious way.

"Never forget those who do not yet know God's love and who need you to bring them to these fountains of grace. Every human heart longs for God's indescribable love, but many seek to fill that longing by means that leave them empty and alone in the end. Not knowing the power of the Cross, they misuse God's gifts and turn to hollow pleasures that promise happiness but ultimately bring pain. Jenna, the world needs you to carry a broken humanity into the transforming rays of God's love. God raises up an army of such souls in every age, for it is God's will that where sin abounds, grace abounds all the more.

"These souls can be found everywhere and in every vocation — in convents and monasteries, in parishes and rectories, in hospitals and nursing homes, in prisons, in family life, in seminaries, in schools, in the business world, indeed everywhere God is loved and worshiped.

They are souls, like Agnes, whose mission is to bring a broken world to the Father's love, drawing upon it over and over again all the power of these holy mysteries. They love God for those who do not yet know how. They believe for those who do not yet have faith. Through their prayers, they bring light into the dark shadows where so many choose to dwell. It is not an easy path, Jenna, and you will encounter fierce opposition, but an ever-growing love for God and for others will be your strength.

"Never underestimate the possibilities born of this prayer. It contains the power of the Gospel itself. Everyone you wrap in its grace will be given more than you will ever know this side of Heaven. Never forget that you, too, are the recipient of such prayers. Since the day you came into her life, Agnes prayed so many Rosaries and offered so much of her suffering on your behalf. She loved you very much, and her sincere love and faith pierced through to the heart of God. Now you are experiencing the fruit of her prayers. This, even more than the rosary you are holding, was Agnes' greatest gift to you. But remember, Jenna" he added, "those who know the power of the Rosary are impelled by love to act on that knowledge." At the angel's final words, she was enveloped by a profound peace.

Jenna's guardian angel got up and stood next to the Christmas tree. A light slowly appeared around him, becoming brighter and brighter until she could no longer see him. Jenna stood up and remained in silence for a moment. Then, rather than feeling sad, she bowed her head in a spontaneous prayer of gratitude for all she had been given. Although she could no longer see or hear him, she knew her guardian angel's arm was draped around her shoulder.

She smiled at the angel's words, still echoing in her head. "More often than you can imagine, Jenna, great graces are granted through the prayers and quiet witness of heroes like Agnes."

Christmas Day had arrived, and tears of joy were streaming down Jenna's face. Agnes had given her more than a Christmas gift. She had given her the gift of Christmas. Pressing Agnes' rosary close to her heart, Jenna went off to get ready to celebrate Christmas like never before, the Christmas when Christ was born in her heart.

Epilogue

Remember not the events of the past,
the things of long ago, consider not;
See, I am doing something new!

Now it springs forth, do you not perceive it?
In the wilderness I make a way,
in the wasteland, rivers
(Isaiah 43:18-19).

"What? You're going to church *now?*" Jenna's mother asked. "Don't you at least want to open your presents first? Dad will be over any minute, and you're the one who insisted he come over first thing Christmas morning."

Then she noticed the rosary beads her daughter was pressing against her heart and the opened box under the tree that had contained Agnes' gift. She looked at Jenna and smiled. "Okay, hold on, I'll drop you off. It's freezing out."

Jenna glanced impatiently at her cell phone to check the time while her mother went to her room to get her purse. "There's a Catholic Church a couple of miles away," her mother yelled from down the corridor. "I used to give Agnes a ride sometimes. I'll take you there. I think it's called Guardian Angels Church." Jenna laughed. *Of course it is.*

She grabbed her black winter coat, red scarf, and gloves from the coat closet. Then she took her mother's hand and pulled her out the front door and towards the car.

***

Jenna arrived about a half hour before Mass. A gentle peace came over her as she took in the sights and sounds of the church bustling with Christmas morning activity. A sea of red poinsettias flanked the altar, which was draped in stark white linens. The sound of Christmas carols and friendly banter floated through the church as the pews quickly filled up.

Jenna took a deep breath. She knew what she had to do. She glanced around the church and saw a young priest setting up for Mass. He looked busy, but she was determined. She marched up to the front of the church and stood at the bottom of the steps leading up to the center of the sanctuary, gripping Agnes' rosary tightly in her hand. As she waited for the priest to notice her, she thought her heart would beat right through her chest.

He finally spotted her and smiled warmly. She was relieved to see that he was friendly. "Hi there," he said coming toward her and extending his hand. "Merry Christmas. I'm Fr. Joe."

"Hi Father, I was wondering if you could hear my Confession."

***

When Jenna exited the confessional twenty minutes later, she felt as though she were walking on air. Fr. Joe accompanied her out and led her straight to the first pew, asking people to push in so Jenna could have a prime spot. "You made my Christmas, Jenna," he whispered in her ear with a radiant smile as she took her seat.

Going back to Confession after seven years hadn't been nearly as awkward as she thought it would be. The priest gently guided her through the whole process, and, when she confessed her sins, she didn't feel judged. He only seemed happy to see her unload so much baggage. When she had finished confessing, he gave her some practical advice and some prayers to say, and then came the beautiful prayer of absolution: *"God the Father of mercies, through the Death and Resurrection of Your Son, You have reconciled the world to Yourself and sent the Holy Spirit among us for the forgiveness of sins. Through the ministry of the Church, may God grant you pardon and peace. And I absolve you of your sins, in the name of the Father, and of the Son and of the Holy Spirit. Amen."*

As she waited for Mass to begin, Jenna thought back to all that had happened the previous night. It seemed like a dream, but she knew it wasn't. The relief she felt after Confession caused her to think of the first disciples in the mystery of the Resurrection, when Jesus appeared to them in the Upper Room and forgave them for abandoning him. Last night she had merely witnessed their relief, but now she was experiencing it.

She closed her eyes and joy flooded her soul. Even though the church was packed, and her guardian angel was, no doubt, close by her side, she felt like she was alone with God. *This is what God and Agnes wanted for me all along,* she thought. *Why did I resist for so many years?*

Although she fumbled through the responses at Mass and couldn't always remember when to sit, stand, or kneel, it felt right to be there. Everything was familiar and yet somehow brand new at the same time.

"Take this, all of you, and eat of it, for this is my Body, which will be given up for you," the priest said, lifting the Sacred Host high above the altar. As Fr. Joe spoke those words, an image from the previous night flashed through her mind. She saw Jesus during his Passion, disfigured from the beatings he received, blood dripping down his face from the crown of thorns upon his head, and his eyes burning with love.

Then something the angel had said suddenly came back to her, as if he were speaking to her anew: "The celebration of the Eucharist does more than simply recall the events of the Last Supper. It makes present the Passion, Death, and Resurrection of Christ, offering their fruit to all who receive. The Mass is Christ's saving work continually re-presented to the Father for humankind, making the grace of these mysteries readily and tangibly accessible to people in every age."

As she knelt in front of her pew after receiving Communion for the first time since her Confirmation two years before, she looked around and wondered how many truly understood what had just happened on that altar. Being at Mass was even more amazing than anything that had happened the night before, because now she was no longer just an observer. She had actually *received* the Lord and entered his saving mysteries. She had the urge to shout this newfound understanding from every rooftop.

***

After Mass, Jenna gradually made her way toward the back of the church, savoring the tangible peace she felt in and around her. Her eyes wandered toward the back corner of the church and suddenly her heart began to pound. She did a double take. There he was, sitting in the back corner, looking directly at her. It had been nearly eighteen months since she last saw him. There were dark circles under his eyes, his light brown hair was longer, and he needed a shave, but it was him. It was definitely Justin.

She ran toward her brother and threw her arms around his neck. He looked around nervously, but after seeing that everyone was too busy wishing friends a Merry Christmas to notice him, his shoulders relaxed and he returned Jenna's embrace.

"What on earth are you doing here?!" she asked, stepping back so she could look at him.

"I just wanted to see you," he replied. "I was sitting in a car across from the new house, hoping to catch you alone. I followed you here and came in after Mom left." Jenna wasn't even aware that he knew where the new house was.

"Please come home, Justin, at least for Christmas dinner," she pleaded.

"Not yet, I'm not ready to face Mom and Dad," he said with firm resolve. Then he added with that impish smile, "So you go to church now?"

"Yeah, well, it's kind of a new thing."

"That's cool. Pray for me, okay? I have to go," he said shifting his weight from side to side. "Promise you won't tell Mom and Dad that you saw me. I'll get there eventually, just not today."

She had to fight the overwhelming urge to wrestle him to the ground to stop him from leaving. She wanted to keep him there and call her parents, but she was afraid if she pushed him into coming home before he was ready, he would only run away again. She reluctantly agreed and promised she would pray for him. She knew this was an opportunity to exercise her newfound faith by trusting God, but it still wasn't easy. Justin left by a side door, and she watched as he turned the corner and vanished from her sight.

Jenna was heading toward the main door and was just about to leave when a voice called from behind. "Hey, Jenna, is that you?"

"Maggie!" Jenna cried. "I didn't know you go to church." Maggie's eyes looked heavy, and Jenna hoped it wasn't because of more bullying.

"Yeah, well, my parents...," she said, rolling her eyes. "Why don't you let us give you ride home so you don't have to wait for your mom?"

As they turned to leave, Jenna spotted a flyer for a youth group retreat. She took two copies and gave one to Maggie. "Fr. Joe told me about this when I went to Confession."

"Confession? What's been going on with you?" Maggie asked, wide-eyed.

Jenna laughed. "It looks interesting. We should check it out."

"My parents would love that. They're always trying to get me to go to youth group."

"It's settled then," she said, promising herself that from now on she would be a real friend for Maggie.

Jenna put her arm around Maggie's shoulder, and they descended the long staircase outside the church. "Everything's going to be okay, Maggie. For both of us."

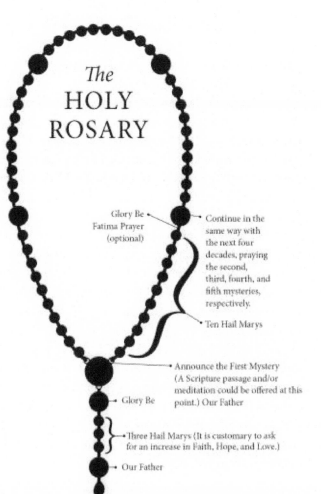

The
HOLY
ROSARY

Glory Be
Fatima Prayer
(optional)

Continue in the
same way with
the next four
decades, praying
the second,
third, fourth, and
fifth mysteries,
respectively.

Ten Hail Marys

Announce the First Mystery
(A Scripture passage and/or
meditation could be offered at this
point.) Our Father

Glory Be

Three Hail Marys (It is customary to ask
for an increase in Faith, Hope, and Love.)

Our Father

Sign of the Cross
Apostles' Creed
(See prayers on the next page)

SIGN OF THE CROSS: In the name of the Father, and of the Son, and of the Holy Spirit. Amen.

APOSTLES' CREED: I believe in God, the Father almighty, Creator of Heaven and Earth, and in Jesus Christ, his only Son, our Lord, who was conceived by the Holy Spirit, born of the Virgin Mary, suffered under Pontius Pilate, was crucified, died and was buried; he descended into Hell; on the third day he rose again from the dead; he ascended into Heaven, and is seated at the right hand of God the Father almighty; from there he will come to judge the living and the dead. I believe in the Holy Spirit, the holy catholic Church, the communion of saints, the forgiveness of sins, the resurrection of the body, and life everlasting. Amen.

OUR FATHER: Our Father, who art in Heaven, hallowed be Thy name; Thy kingdom come; Thy will be done on Earth as it is in Heaven. Give us this day our daily bread; and forgive us our trespasses as we forgive those who trespass against us; and lead us not into temptation, but deliver us from evil. Amen.

HAIL MARY: Hail Mary, full of grace, the Lord is with thee; blessed art thou among women, and blessed is the fruit of thy womb, Jesus. Holy Mary, Mother of God, pray for us sinners now and at the hour of our death. Amen

GLORY BE: Glory be to the Father, and to the Son, and to the Holy Spirit; as it was in the beginning, is now, and ever shall be, world without end. Amen.

FATIMA PRAYER (optional prayer between decades): O My Jesus, forgive us our sins, save us from the fires of Hell and lead all souls to Heaven, especially those who are in most need of Thy mercy.

HAIL, HOLY QUEEN: Hail, holy Queen, Mother of Mercy, our life, our sweetness, and our hope! To thee do we cry, poor banished children of Eve; to thee do we send up our sighs, mourning and weeping in this valley of tears. Turn then, most gracious Advocate, thine eyes of mercy toward us; and after this our exile, show unto us the blessed fruit of thy womb, Jesus; O clement, O loving, O sweet Virgin Mary.

(Verse): Pray for us, O Holy Mother of God.
(Response): That we may be made worthy of the promises of Christ.

ROSARY PRAYER
(Verse): Let us pray,
(Response): O God, whose only begotten Son has purchased for us the rewards of eternal life, grant we beseech Thee, that while meditating upon these mysteries of the Most Holy Rosary of the Blessed Virgin Mary, we may both imitate what they contain and obtain what they promise, through the same Christ our Lord. Amen.

THE MYSTERIES OF THE ROSARY

THE JOYFUL MYSTERIES (Monday & Saturday)
1. The Annunciation
2. The Visitation
3. The Nativity
4. The Presentation of Jesus in the Temple
5. The Finding of Jesus in the Temple

THE LUMINOUS MYSTERIES (Thursday)
1. The Baptism of the Lord
2. The Miracle at Cana
3. The Proclamation of the Kingdom
4. The Transfiguration
5. The Institution of the Eucharist

THE SORROWFUL MYSTERIES (Tuesday & Friday)
1. The Agony in the Garden
2. The Scourging at the Pillar
3. The Crowning with Thorns
4. The Carrying of the Cross
5. The Crucifixion

THE GLORIOUS MYSTERIES (Wednesday & Sunday)
1. The Resurrection
2. The Ascension
3. The Descent of the Holy Spirit
4. The Assumption of Mary
5. The Coronation of Mary

A Few Quotes on the Rosary

The Rosary is a school of prayer. The Rosary is a school of faith. *Pope Francis*

With the Rosary, in fact, we allow ourselves to be guided by Mary, the model of faith, in meditating on the mysteries of Christ, and day after day we are helped to assimilate the Gospel so that it shapes all our lives.
Pope Benedict XVI

The Rosary is my favorite prayer. A marvelous prayer! Marvelous in its simplicity and its depth.
St. John Paul II

The Most Holy Virgin in these last times in which we live has given a new efficacy to the recitation of the Rosary to such an extent that there is no problem, no matter how difficult it is, whether temporal or above all spiritual, in the personal life of each one of us, of our families...that cannot be solved by the Rosary. There is no problem, I tell you, no matter how difficult it is, that we cannot resolve by the prayer of the Holy Rosary.
Sr. Lucia dos Santos, Fatima seer

Go to the Madonna. Love her! Always say the Rosary. Say it well. Say it as often as you can! Be souls of prayer. Never tire of praying, it is what is essential. Prayer shakes the Heart of God, it obtains necessary graces!
St. Pio of Pietreclina

The holy Rosary is a powerful weapon. Use it with confidence and you'll be amazed at the results.
St. Josemaria Escriva

The Rosary is the book of the blind, where souls see and there enact the greatest drama of love the world has ever known; it is the book of the simple, which initiates them into mysteries and knowledge more satisfying than the education of other men; it is the book of the aged, whose eyes close upon the shadow of this world, and open on the substance of the next. The power of the rosary is beyond description. *Venerable Fulton Sheen*

There is no surer means of calling down God's blessings upon the family... than the daily recitation of the Rosary.
Pope Venerable Pius XII

The Rosary is a long chain that links Heaven and Earth. One end of it is in our hands and the other end is in the hands of the Holy Virgin. *St. Therese of Lisieux*

Among all the devotions approved by the Church, none has been so favored by so many miracles as the devotion of the Most Holy Rosary. *Blessed Pope Pius IX*

Never will anyone who says his Rosary every day be led astray. This is a statement that I would gladly sign with my blood. *St. Louis de Montfort*

The Holy Rosary is the storehouse of countless blessings.
Blessed Alan de la Roche

Download your *free*

Rosary Meditations,

based on *Agnes' Gift*, today!

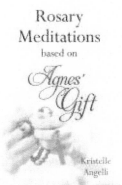

Go to:
KristelleAngelli.com/meditations,
and follow the simple instructions.

Thank you for reading *Agnes' Gift!* I hope you enjoyed reading it as much as I enjoyed writing it. Please consider leaving a short review on Amazon. Simply go to the Product Details Page for *Agnes' Gift* and click "Write a customer review" in the Customer Reviews Section. Then click "Submit."

If you wish to contact the author, you can do so through one of the following ways:

Kristelle Angelli

John Paul Publishing

PO Box 283

Tewksbury, MA 01876

Website: KristelleAngelli.com

Email: kristelle@kristelleangelli.com

Facebook: @KristelleAngelliAuthor

If you would like to be notified of new releases, please sign up for updates at KristelleAngelli.com/updates.

ABOUT THE AUTHOR

 Kristelle Angelli has worked in young adult ministry since 2000. She is currently the Catholic Campus Minister at Emerson College, Boston, and Framingham State University. Kristelle holds a Master of Arts in Christian Ministry from St. John's Seminary, Brighton, MA, and a Bachelor of Arts in Print Journalism from St. Michael's College, Winooski, VT.

When she is not working, Kristelle enjoys Taekwon-do, or can be found kayaking or snowshoeing near her home in Tewksbury, MA.